LIPS LIKE SUGAR

LIPS LIKE SUGAR
WOMEN'S EROTIC FANTASIES

EDITED BY
VIOLET BLUE

FOREWORD BY
THOMAS S. ROCHE

Published in the United States by Cleis Press, Inc.,
2246 Sixth St., Berkeley, California 9710.

Printed in the United States.
Cover design: Scott Idleman/Blink
Cover photograph: Nina K. Sundberg/Getty Images
Text design: Frank Wiedemann
Second Edition.
10 9 8 7 6 5 4 3 2 1

Print ISBN: 978-1-57344-820-8
E-Book ISBN: 978-1-57344-834-5

"Cops and Robbers" by KC first appeared in *Best Bondage Erotica*, edited by Alison Tyler (Cleis Press, 2003).

Contents

FOREWORD: HOOKED ON FANTASIES

Sharing fantasies was one of the first sexual things I ever did. My first girlfriend Bianca insisted on it.

The daughter of a pro-pleasure '60s feminist nurse-midwife, Bianca had a broad-minded attitude about fantasies. Hers included a lot of Tim Curry as Frank-N-Furter from *The Rocky Horror Picture Show*, plus sometimes Columbia and Magenta. But even more often, she fantasized about David Bowie. Bowie, in particular, was fond of tying her up: "So I can't get away," she told me. "So I *have* to let Bowie pleasure me."

Sometimes there was a gag involved, so she couldn't even complain about Bowie eating her out—because, seriously, wouldn't that be any woman's first impulse if David Bowie started going down on her?

It was the middle of the '80s—when, in our world, New Wave was king and a college-prep flavor of Punk was its attitudinal cousin. Bianca told me these fantasies proudly: proud because the fantasies were her creations and she was a creative person at heart—but also because they were out on the edge. *Screw the Normals* was a prominent guiding principle for her, as it was for many of my friends in those years.

One of Bianca's non-bondage Bowie fantasies involved the B-man laboring over some "Lady Stardust"-style piano riff, and being unable to find the right note. Bianca comes up behind him wearing a split-side, thigh-baring Elvira dress and gives him the longed-for B-flat—one perfect note to complete the perfect riff...rendered with her stiletto heel just before she grabs Bowie's mullet and rams his face into her crotch.

Bianca didn't want royalties or a coauthor credit for her contribution...just a perfect tongue-job from Ziggy Stardust in lieu of fame and fortune. No ropes necessary this time, because he *owes* her, right?

Bianca's piano fantasy tangles up dreams of creativity and sex. In late adolescence at the time, Bianca was fantasizing about what teenage girls are "supposed" to fantasize about—musicians and actors. But she was also fantasizing about her own actualization, her own power, her own significance, her own chance to express herself on par with the sparkle-booted guy who had rocked her world. Many of us find our erotic fixations forming early in our sexual lives. Some of those interests stick with us indefinitely, even if they only make occasional appearances. It's only natural that many of us feel young in our fantasies—and that in sexual fantasy, we're given permission for our obsessions to be "immature." That's why fantasies are so unbelievably private and sharing them so unbelievably intimate. Women don't get shy and embarrassed and sometimes a little ashamed about sharing fantasies just because they're "dirty." Sometimes they're silly; they're cheesy; they're goofy. They reveal things deeper than "just" what turns us on. Sexual fantasies reveal what drives us on every level.

Women's sexual fantasies are about more than just the sexual response cycle; they're about *creativity*. Everybody, even people who make their living being creative, need somewhere to go and just *dream*.

Contrary to pop-psychology proclamations, women's sexual fantasies can be as down and dirty as men's. They can be as simple and sex-focused, as dick-focused, as cunt-focused, as talk-dirty-to-me, as how-nasty-can-you-be, as shut-the-fuck-up-and-fucking-fuck-me as any scenario from the mouth of some swaggering, cocky bastard...and, incidentally, it might be just such an imagined cocky bastard who sashays up in cowboy boots and a sneer and starts spewing dirty words.

Some pop-psychology types are inclined to question whether women's fantasies are more "complicated" than men's. Are they more subtle, more "dynamic-focused," less visual? I haven't got the foggiest idea...but I know women's fantasies are hot, surprising, even shocking; they're sometimes visual, sometimes dynamic-focused, sometimes simple-as-hell...and even when they're simple, they're unquestionably complicated.

Not everybody can live the life of a fantasy-fueling sex symbol, obviously; not everybody even gets to be an also-ran in a rock star's list of sexual conquests. And not every woman gets to cowrite a song with one strategically-placed stiletto heel and then get eaten out by David Bowie.

Except that she does, if she wants—in the vast, gorgeous, "complicated" land of sexual fantasy.

Giving voice to sexual fantasy is liberating, yes. It's inspiring, sure. But it's far more than that. Sexual fantasy is downright *spiritual*.

I'm not a man inclined to make bold paranormal pronouncements about the *Spiritus Mundi*, and I don't believe in any one universal definition of love. But if there's an energetic side to human cognition, it's made up of equal parts compassion, affection and lust. Whatever connections we make with other people, we're all alone in our brains much of the time. There, most, if not all, of us are routinely visited by dirty thoughts that throw our hearts and minds into a tailspin. For many of us, those naughty thoughts and taboo impulses sometimes seem like they came from somewhere totally alien—outside us, and outside any form of human reason. If you're a dedicated indulger in your own sexual fantasies, and especially if you're a devotee of self-pleasure, there's a chance you've had the experience of having your fantasy take a sudden left turn that leaves you reeling—and dangerously aroused.

Why the hell did that *occur to me*? you might think.

It's a fair question, but one that's usually damned hard to answer.

Where do women's sexual fantasies come from?

Somewhere deep, somewhere dark, somewhere magical.

The first time I heard Bianca tell me one, I was hooked on women's sexual fantasies. I've been hooked ever since.

I hope the hot, heady, dirty, dangerous fantasies in *Lips Like Sugar* hook you not just on these women's sexual fantasies—but on your own.

Thomas S. Roche
Salt Lake City, Utah

INTRODUCTION: THE WORLD IN A KISS

The way I see it, having a sexual fantasy isn't that different from being on vacation. If you prefer, you can spend the entire time on your back (in the sun). You might get caught up in a compromising airport search for a few hours. It could be that you prefer active vacations, from water sports to pole climbing. Or decadent parties might be your idea of a getaway, uniforms and handcuffs optional. And if getting closer to nature is your fantasy escape, you can always find a few wild animals on the beach. Of course, the alleyways and bars of your own hometown might be where you get away from it all, or you could become a tour guide, leading the men and women of the world astray. All while working on your tan, of course.

It never fails to surprise me that the most-current books on women's sexual fantasies constantly cited in the press and so-called women's magazines are about thirty years old. But they are that old: No one's bothered, or had the courage, to update our fantasy destinations. To me, that's like using a Venice guidebook from 1975 to plan your summer 2012 vacation. Not just any old map will do—not if you want to see the canals from as many vantage points as possible.

When I go on vacation, as when I have a sexual fantasy, I want to see as many unexplored, unimaginable destinations as possible. I don't just want to be a passenger on a safe ride—I want to do, see, and feel things that I can't find at home. Or maybe I want to try them at home; either way, I don't want the ride to be boring.

The authors in *Lips Like Sugar* agree, and they bring us a shocking, arousing, and unflinchingly explicit tour of women's sexual fantasies, all with a twist, and told to us with lips like…well, like something sweet. In "Quick Fix" by Heather Peltier, we follow an on-the-go businesswoman as she demands a lunchtime tryst from her contractor husband, only to get more than she bargained for on a busy work site. Similarly, "The 9.30 to Edinburgh" by Carolina John takes a routine train journey with a woman who observes—and then participates in—some outrageous but not unbelievable ways to pass the time. "When I Make You Say No" by Julia Price goes to a different destination altogether, to the point of no return when a man, any man, is brought to the edge of saying "no" to the woman who is having her way with him, and then he's pushed just a bit further. Zoe Bishop's "Crazy from the Heat" is a day at the beach, with two women who take toying with the men who are watching them a little further than they expected, but then decide to enjoy their public Sapphic experiments for just themselves.

Like her male cultural counterpart, the powerful businessman who visits the dominatrix for submissive release, the woman in J. Sinclaire's "Teddy" seeks nothing more than an expert male hand to take away that power in the bedroom, though the results of this tale are deliciously more realistic than the businessman's fantasy. In "The Accidental Exhibitionist" by Debra Hyde, unintended exhibitionism is just the beginning for the woman who lets her boyfriend call the shots at a BDSM play party. "Jen and Tim" by Kay Jaybee visit a different kind of party altogether where costumes are the dish of the day, but Tim gets a special strap-on surprise for dessert, and the author knows how to serve up a nice, explicit bombshell, albeit well hidden under a uniform.

Tsaurah Litzky's "Discipline" isn't merely your typical drug- and alcohol-soaked bad-boys-in-the-band memoir, and our female protagonist has the irony and wit to see the whole bizarre experience through to a satisfying finish. "The Power of Imagination" by BJ Franklin takes the delirium of one woman's erotic fantasies to the limits, while in Dara Prisamt Murray's "Airport Security" a taboo fantasy many of us have held privately after passing through an airport becomes startling reality for one lucky woman, limits passed at the check-in counter, thank you very much.

When fantasy is the beauty and the lyricism found in the cat-and-mouse game of seduction, A. D. R. Forte's "Endymion" takes us there, and we see that taking a workmate down the forbidden path can be as wistful, enjoyable, and nasty as we want it to be. Alyssa Brooks delivers a tale of boundaries and limits surpassed with forceful, though highly desired, group abduction sex in "Callie's Kidnapping." And "The Guy Your Mother Warned You About" by Chris Costello provides deliciously sticky insight on having your way with a woman of a different kind, proving that genderfuck and butch-femme dynamics can be a lot of fun when the fantasy doesn't go the way you planned it.

We've all done it at some point—shown up at a party in the

wrong outfit. But in KC's "Cops and Robbers," what seems to be one girl's ridiculously poorly planned, high-concept costume turns out to be just the thing to get her into the trouble she craves. On the topic of cravings, Ayre Riley's "Mr. Right(s)" begins in a place many of us have been—at the breakup end of singlehood—but takes a twist when our female hero puts a few men in their place with her rapacious sexual appetite. "Force of Nature," delivered expertly by Miranda Austin, tries to tuck us in for a night of restful sleep, but once our female alter-ego is awakened by a burglar, all bets for a restful night of sleep are off.

It's easy to look at the title of Erica Dumas's story "The First Stroke" and think it's a BDSM tale, but after our heroine utters her first "suck my dick" to her shocked boyfriend, we see she's definitely stroking her beat to a different drummer. Erin Sanders, with a hilarious yet all-too-good list of "Erin's Rules" for her sexual submission and behavior to her lover, makes us wonder, "Does she?" But in the end, we're swept away to the shores of Croatia and back in Teresa Lamai's "Idyll," in which a trio of young adult refugees find solace in sexual experimentation and long afternoons filled with memories.

This book is about escaping the known and the ordinary in the world of women's sexual fantasies, and in the world of erotica by and for women. The chances these women take, the impulses they act on, and the forbidden taboos they explore on their own terms are experiences you will not find in any other collection for women. These fantasies are fierce, fearless, unapologetic—and utterly, enjoyably sublime. The women who wrote the stories collected here didn't need to travel to Italy; they just looked in the most strange, outrageous, and undeniably arousing places they could think of: within the contours of their own sexual imaginings. Use this book as you would any other sex toy—or travel guide. Read it alone, read it aloud to your lover, or mark your favorite story and leave it as a surprise for someone who's ready for a getaway.

Violet Blue
San Francisco

QUICK FIX

Heather Peltier

I don't know why; sometimes it just happens. Some fluctuation of my hormones or something that makes me think about you all morning. I'm squirming at my desk, feeling that tingling all over my body that tells me that if I don't satisfy the need building inside me, I'm going to go absolutely crazy.

Normally, I hold it. I mean, I just put it out of my mind, bringing it back out between meetings, when I'm sitting at my desk answering voice mail messages. I sit there and think about you while some lower-level manager is telling me her problems, blathering on about one thing or another. I sit there and get wet thinking about you, but I don't do anything about it. I don't rush home and fuck you, no matter how badly I want to.

This time, though, I can't sit still. I can't handle it. Sitting in meetings, all I can think about is you: your lips, pressed against mine; your tongue, pressing urgently into my mouth; your chest, thrusting hard against me, teasing my nipples with your soft hair; and, most importantly, your glorious cock sliding between my lips while I kneel in front of you or sinking deep into me as you enter me.

I call you on your cell phone. I know you'll answer, because you're on a job, in the middle of construction on a half-million dollar home up in the hills.

"Are you free for lunch?" I ask you breathlessly.

"Sure," you say. "Everyone else is going down to the deli, but I can meet you someplace."

Our home is more than twenty minutes away, but the construction site is only ten. "No," I tell you. "Stay right where you are. Give me the address."

"I'm a little tight on time," you say. "We'll have to go somewhere close."

"I'll bring something to eat," I tell you.

"Oh, a picnic," you say.

"You could say that."

I call my client's cell phone and cancel our lunch meeting.

Hit with pangs of guilt, I grab an apple off my desk and stuff it into the pocket of my business suit. I make a quick stop in the restroom, race out the door of my office, and hop into my car.

Seven minutes later, I find you sitting on the unfinished wooden steps of the house, reading a paperback.

"Hi," you smile. "Did you bring food?"

"I brought something to eat," I tell you, taking your hand. "Is anyone else here?"

"Everyone else is down at the deli," you say, looking at me suspiciously. "What are you up to?"

I walk into the construction site, seeing you start to say something. You've said it before: I'm not on your payroll, so you're risking serious insurance consequences if you let me on your site. But this time, I'm not taking no for an answer.

"Nice place you've got here," I say, walking through what I suppose will be the entryway. Most of the walls are nothing more than two-by-fours, unfinished plywood nail-gunned up to keep the vagrants out. I walk deeper into the house-in-progress and find the kitchen.

You're tagging along behind me. I shrug off my blazer and toss it on a sawdust-covered belt sander. I reach up and unclip my hair, letting it fall in a dark curtain all around my shoulders and face as I run my fingers through it.

"Hey," you say. "You really shouldn't be hanging out in here...."

I turn around and face you, smiling.

"I don't intend to hang out anywhere," I say, and slowly unzip my conservative navy-blue skirt.

It falls in a pool around my feet, and I step out of it.

On my top half, I'm now wearing only my skintight pale-yellow camisole, no bra underneath. I'm small enough that I don't need to wear one—as long as I don't take off my blazer. Now that it's off, I can feel the cool air of the dark construction site brushing my nipples, which are standing out, peaked and firm, aching. On my bottom half, I'm wearing only a pair of lace-top white stockings, hitched to my garter belt with thin white garters and businesslike navy pumps with three-inch heels. My pussy, feeling slick and messy with the juice of wanting you, is bare. My panties are tucked in the top drawer of my desk. I removed them before coming over.

"I need a quick fix," I tell you, reaching between my legs and gently teasing my pussy. "Very quick."

Glancing around, you see that we're close to several open areas that passersby might be able to see through. You look from me to the street, then to me again.

I lift my hand to my face, slipping my finger into my mouth.

I've been playing with my pussy and it tastes like me. And you know it. I lick my finger sensuously, and that's all it takes. You come for me.

I'm down on my knees before you reach me. I've got your filthy, paint-stained work pants open in a split second, and I reach in to pull out your cock. When I take it into my mouth, it's only half-hard. By the time it reaches the back of my throat, it's hard all the way.

I feel a quiver go through you as I swallow your cock. You moan softly as I pump it into me, feeling the sawdust and fragments of plasterboard abrading my knees, tearing my stockings. The roughness of the environment turns me on even more, as do the smell of fresh sawdust and the street noise so close to us, making me feel exposed and vulnerable as I suck you. Vulnerable to humiliation, because I know if you get caught you'll be in big, big trouble. Supervisor or not, you're not supposed to be doing that. That knowledge sends a surge of excitement through me as your hips begin to rock back and forth, pushing your cock deeper into my mouth, deeper into my throat. I caress your balls with my fingers, coaxing you into greater thrusts, fucking me as I kneel in front of you.

You grasp my hair and pull me back gently; my mouth keeps working, inches from your glistening cockhead, my tongue aching to touch you more, my throat open and hungry for your shaft. I look up at you, at your beautiful dark eyes.

"I'm going to come if you don't stop," you tell me. "I want you on the counter."

You gesture toward the skeletal beginnings of a built-in kitchen island. Obediently, I stand up and bend over it, leaning fully on it so my legs leave the ground and my ass hovers in the air, my legs dangling helplessly and my pussy exposed. Now that I'm higher, off the ground, I'm acutely aware of the unfinished windows, bare emptiness facing what will be the back yard, what will be the side. The street noise excites me; almost anyone could look in, if they just walked onto the unprotected site.

"Close your eyes," you tell me, and I do.

I'm full of surprises; I guess you know that. But I don't think I gave you enough credit for being the same, because what I feel next sends a shiver through my body.

You've grabbed some rope. You wrap it around my wrist and start to tie me to the island.

I hear myself gasping; I feel my whole body tensing as I realize that you've pushed this so much further than I intended to go. I feel the sharp pang of fear deep in my body giving rise to a slow pulse of desire as I feel you quickly, expertly knotting the rope around my wrists, tying me to the skeletal frame of the unfinished kitchen island. I don't struggle at first; I feel safe with you. Then, when I test the bonds and feel how tight you've tied them, I feel a rush of excitement and fear mingling deep in my pussy. It floods wet and I can practically feel it dripping down my inner thighs. When I pull against the bonds, squirming and struggling, you grab firm hold of my leg and that excites me more. Forcing my legs apart, you quickly tie first one ankle, then the other, to the framework of the island.

When I test the bonds again, I find myself immobile. I'm helpless, bent over, ass in the air, spread, vulnerable. Anyone could walk in here and have me. And you know it.

As I squirm, I feel my hard nipples rubbing against the rough plywood under me. They hurt a little from the roughness, but strangely I don't mind it. I want it more. The more I squirm, the more my nipples ache and tingle. Meanwhile, I feel your hand on my ass—and it's not empty. You're holding a sander.

You barely press at all as you draw the sandpaper slowly down the backs of my thighs, then over my smooth, slim ass. I catch my breath, overwhelmed with sensation: the dusty smell of the ropes, the sharp tang of sawdust and plywood, the scent of your sweat-soaked, unwashed body, the sound of the street so close by, the cool breeze through the open framework of the house. The heat of my pussy as you bend close to me and put your mouth against the back of my neck.

"I've been wondering how to reward my men for working so hard," you growl into my ear, and my back stiffens, my pussy flooding with heat as you torment me. I feel one hand grinding the sandpaper very lightly against my ass and thighs, the other hand pressing against my pussy and clit. Two fingers enter me, and I gasp. "A monetary bonus just didn't seem like it would satisfy them. How kind of you to provide the perfect reward for a hard day's work."

The heat rises in my pussy as I push back onto you, your fingers pumping me as your growl intensifies, your breath hot and the smell of your sweat close in my nostrils.

"How about if I just leave you here and let them use you for as long as they like? We wouldn't get much work done this afternoon, but I'm sure they'd work twice as hard tomorrow."

I moan softly, writhing in the bonds, pushing back onto you as hard as I can as you finger-fuck me. Your cock still juts out of your open pants, still moist with my spittle, still hard. When you ease your fingers out of my pussy and toss the sandpaper away, I know what's coming.

"Think you could handle that?" you ask me. "There are fifteen of them."

That sends a shiver through me as you position yourself behind me, your cock finding the slick furrow between my pussy lips without delay. You enter me in one hard thrust, and I'm so open I take all of you, gasping as the curve of your cock hits my G-spot. I squirm and try to press back onto you, but your weight bears me down, and the bonds keep me firmly in place. As you start to pound me, my nipples rub raw against the plywood, through the thin silk of my camisole. My hips press into the edge of the wood; I can feel my flesh scraping, but I'm not worrying about splinters. I'm imagining all your workmen fucking me, even as your cock begins to plumb my depths faster and faster with each thrust.

"Come on," you sigh. "You don't mind contributing a little extra to the family business, do you, honey?"

Your cock is hitting exactly the right spot; it always does when you fuck me in this position. From behind, I mean—you've never fucked me in a construction site while I'm bent over a half-done counter. But you know what angle is the perfect one to shove your cock into me, and your cockhead is rubbing me in just the right place to make me—

Come.

But I don't, yet, not quite; you seem to sense I'm closing in on it and slow down just enough to keep me hovering on the edge.

"Say you'll do it, honey," you say, tormenting me with the slowness of your thrusts. "Say you'll let my men use you."

I want to come so bad I would say anything to make you fuck me harder. "Oh god," I gasp. "Of course I will. Of course I will. Anything you want."

"All of them?"

"All of them," I whimper, straining against the bonds and trying to force myself back onto your cock, harder. "Every last one. I'll fuck them all...oh god—"

You start pounding into me again, the head of your cock striking my G-spot in exactly the way it takes to send me over the edge. You grip my slender thighs and hold me down as you ravage me, your cock pumping deep into my cunt and wrenching my orgasm from me.

"Oh god," I moan. "I'm going to—"

Then I do, uncontrollably, your cock savaging me with every thrust, invading me, possessing me. I come so hard my eyes go dim, my whole body goes numb except my exploding clit, my throbbing pussy. I moan, helpless, not even caring who on the street can hear me, bound and naked, getting fucked in a kitchen where rich people will make their California Cuisine. Toward the end I hear myself screaming, as the intensity of my orgasm gets to be more than I can handle. And still you pound me, forcing me to handle it, forcing me to take it, forcing me to experience the most intense orgasm of my life. An orgasm so intense I'm afraid, for a moment, I'm going to pass out.

Then I hear you moaning, feel your cock clenching, feel the thick flood of semen that spells your release. I moan softly, savoring the feel of wetness that comes when you fill me. I lie there, immobile, bent over, exposed, bound—your slave. A bonus for your men, or whoever else you want to possess me.

You slip out of my pussy, your cock softening in its postcoital satisfaction. A thin stream of your come starts to leak down my thigh; it makes me shiver to feel it.

You make short work of the knots on my wrists and ankles. You help me down off the counter and hand me my skirt. My arms go around you and you hug me close, kissing the top of my head.

"What," I say. "No bonus for your men?"

"Nope," you tell me. "I'm keeping this one all to myself."

THE 9.30 TO EDINBURGH

Carolina John

Alison didn't usually travel first class. But the timetable informed her that the journey from London to Edinburgh was going to be exceptionally long, and, if her past experience of train journeys was anything to go by, exceptionally tedious. So she thought she'd treat herself to a bit of luxury for a change, especially since she'd been working hard all week and hadn't had a break from the city for six months. Now she felt that she deserved to pamper herself a little.

Besides, the train company that had recently bought the line was particularly concerned with the business of attracting customers—especially the kind who could afford to pay extra for a better class of service. Consequently the train company was pioneering a return to luxury compartment carriages for long journeys, restricted to first class passengers, of course. And when Alison saw the pictures in the brochure depicting comfortable seats in spotless air-conditioned compartments with adjustable lighting, personal stereo, and plenty of leg room, she handed over the extortionate fare without demur. It would be good to have a change from the clinical, brightly lit carriages that held sixty people and didn't allow the passengers room to stretch their legs out under the narrow tables. And a small, cozy compartment would be much more intimate—if the right person got on the train to share it with her.

She'd managed to avoid going up to Edinburgh at Christmas and the Millennium—so she'd actually saved some money by waiting until she had a good reason to visit her family. And hearing Aunt Moira's will being read by her solicitor was a very good reason indeed—especially when she thought that she might just inherit a few thousand pounds at the very time when she desperately needed some cash. Alison wasn't exactly broke, but her money was "tied up" in various lucrative but complicated business ventures that she knew would eventually reap rewards but that didn't allow her the freedom to spend what she wanted when she wanted to. The trouble was that Alison was the type of woman who needed rewards immediately.

Alison was a NOW person.

At twenty-four she reckoned she'd had enough of saving for what she wanted in life. Now she should be able to have what she wanted when she wanted it. And that went for everything—clothes, holidays, clubbing, meals out, and of course, men. She'd thought that she wanted Mike. Probably because he'd flashed his money around and had bought her all the other things that she'd also wanted. But now she had grown tired of him, and part of her yearned for a change of partner. Someone exciting who didn't treat sex as though it was an activity you had to indulge in once a week in the missionary position when the lights were out.

"Fuck me!" she had once screamed at him at two o'clock in the afternoon.

"Don't be crude, Alison," he had replied coldly. "I'll make love to you later—when we're in bed."

Alison had read stories in which the heroine was shagged everywhere, including the kitchen sink—and she craved the excitement of an impromptu liaison in an unusual place. The idea of a good fuck on the train appealed to her, but it didn't seem likely in reality. How many people would really take advantage of a situation like that? This wasn't a paperback novel—this was reality.

Mike hadn't liked the idea of her going to Edinburgh without him. But then, Mike didn't like the idea of her doing anything that might exclude him. Family business excluded him because he didn't know her family. Alison would have excluded him anyway—because she didn't want his "I-know-it-all" interference. He was arrogant, boring, and predictable—and when she came back, if she came back richer, she would dump him once and for all. In truth, it was only his money that attracted her. His stupidity in believing that she was in love with him had enabled her to use his money to finance her beautiful Belgravia flat in her own name, in effect signing his departure from her life. Alison was intelligent and sharp as a razor, and she needed an attractive man whom she couldn't fool. She needed someone as astute as herself. Anyone foolish enough to let her get the better of him deserved her contempt, in her opinion.

Unfortunately, today, as she had predicted, there were no intelligent and attractive men on the 9.30 to Edinburgh. In fact, to her annoyance, she had the compartment completely to herself. And so she opened her fashion magazine and sat back to read it, half-contented with her own company and yet half-yearning for male company. Outside the window the countryside flashed past in a blur of greens, greys, and browns—dull, predictable, and unattractive.

Like Mike.

She sighed. If something exciting didn't happen soon, then this was going to be one hell of a boring journey, she thought sadly.

And then her predictions were proved wrong. Attractive excitement suddenly arrived at Birmingham's New Street Station. And for Alison nothing would ever be the same again.

The man and woman who entered her compartment oozed sex appeal and intelligence. Before they entered she heard the pleasant, educated voices in the corridor outside her compartment and she was delighted when they stopped at the sliding door. At last, she thought. Someone to talk to! But, with her usual coolness, she pretended to be engrossed in her magazine as they came in, looking at them surreptitiously from beneath her dark lashes. Her first impression was dark suits, Monsieur Rochas cologne, and expensive perfume. She also noticed that he carried a copy of the *Financial Times* and she hefted a black leather briefcase.

"Do you mind if we join you?" The woman's voice was throaty and sensual, and she looked every inch the professional businesswoman in her tailored pin-striped suit with a knee-length skirt and soft, grey silk blouse. She smiled, flashing a set of pearly whites that any Hollywood dentist would be proud of. Alison smiled back.

"Not at all," she replied. "I was beginning to think that this was a ghost train." The woman's companion smiled and nodded slowly.

"I've thought the same thing every time I've travelled on this line," he said, looking straight into her eyes. Alison's heart missed a beat. He was everything that she'd ever thought attractive in a man—tall, dark, muscular, and intense. His hair was very short and his wide, mysterious eyes were the colour of rich milk chocolate. As they bore into her flesh she shivered with excitement, self-consciously smoothing her long chestnut hair back from her forehead. This man exuded exoticism and passion, she thought. It was a pity that he was with his—wife? Girlfriend? Well, it was just tragic that he had another woman with him. Alison crossed a nylon-clad leg and ran her fingers over her thighs, glad that she had worn the black silk skirt that clung flatteringly to her figure, enhancing the curves of her buttocks. He looked at her legs and flicked his tongue over his lips. She hoped that he had glimpsed the lacy tops of her stockings as she had slid one leg across the other. It might just make him wonder what else she was wearing. Her pale-green blouse was slightly see-through, and she noted with satisfaction that the stranger was now staring longingly at her breasts. Perhaps his companion was just a business colleague, she hoped. One thing was sure, though—Alison wanted this man sexually. Really wanted him.

"You're a regular traveller, then?" she asked as he took the seat opposite hers and placed his companion's briefcase under the window.

"Yes," he replied. "Sarah and I often have to visit clients in Scotland." He cast a glance to his blonde companion and Alison's heart leaped as she realised that she was, as she had hoped, just a colleague. "But after a while travelling can become really tedious—and we do all we can to try to make the journey as interesting as possible," he added. Sarah nodded, her eyes flashing knowingly at her companion before settling on Alison's hot face.

"Absolutely. And I can honestly say that we've had more than our fair share of fun on some of the journeys. Outrageous fun, in fact." She glanced meaningfully at her companion and then back to Alison. "This is Max, by the way. And you are—?"

"Alison. Pleased to meet you, Max and—Sarah, is it?"

Sarah smiled warmly and nodded, then glanced out the window. The train was pulling away from the station and nobody else had entered their compartment.

"It looks as though we're alone until York," she said. "The train doesn't stop again until then." Max grinned.

"I wonder what we can do to amuse ourselves for three and a half hours?" he mused, his long, tapered fingers drumming restlessly on his lap.

"Max hates to be bored," explained Sarah to Alison, who was finding it increasingly difficult to drag her eyes away from the man opposite, who was now staring moodily out the window. For a moment he reminded Alison of Heathcliffe in *Wuthering Heights*—dark, handsome, brooding. Then Sarah went on, "Sometimes I have to help him to amuse himself," she added, turning to him and beginning to stroke his thigh. "Isn't that right, Max?" Max nodded.

"Quite right," he agreed. "And you always do it so beautifully Sarah. Like now. Did I ever tell you that you have a wonderful touch?"

"Many times, darling," she murmured.

He closed his eyes and Alison watched as Sarah's hand moved farther and farther up his leg, stroking slowly and sensually until it reached his groin. Her eyes widened. Surely they weren't going to start groping each other right in front of her? These were respectable business colleagues, she thought. Any minute now they would realise that what they were doing was just not socially acceptable.

"This helps him to relax, Alison," murmured Sarah apologetically as she began to caress his penis over the well-cut dark grey trousers. "But this helps him even more." With one deft movement she unzipped his fly and slid her hand into the opening, where it remained, caressing and teasing the penis that was hidden from Alison, but that she suddenly wanted desperately to see. She could just make out the outline of it, long and fat. Much bigger than Mike's. She gasped. This had happened to her in dreams before—but had never even been hinted at in reality.

"You don't object if Sarah helps me to relax?" asked Max.

"No! No, of course not," stammered Alison, her eyes transfixed by the hand that was moving up and down beneath the fabric of Max's trousers. Once or twice she thought she caught a glimpse of flesh and her heart jumped. A familiar wetness began to form in the gusset of her panties and she felt a flutter in her breast. Hardly aware of what she was doing, she leaned forward slightly, her mouth hanging open a bit and her eyes wide with curiosity. Her face began to burn and she was sure that she must be blushing, but even so she couldn't tear her eyes away. She was appalled—and yet she was fascinated. She wanted them to stop doing what they were doing—and yet if they had stopped she would have been more disappointed than she had ever been in her life.

Sarah's fingers kept moving and Max began to groan with pleasure. He squirmed on the seat and his eyes were dark with passion. His hand moved to his waistband and a moment later he had undone the button of his trousers, so that they opened wide, revealing navy-blue underpants. Still Sarah rubbed and caressed him and as Alison watched, the tip of his penis began to appear between the folds of his zip. She gasped as she feasted her eyes on the shiny, bulbous end, which moved through Sarah's fingers as easily as if it had been oiled. As the foreskin slid up and down he began to moan.

"Not so fast, Sarah. Slow down. Maybe you should stop doing this. What will Alison think?"

"I don't know," replied Sarah. "What do you think, Alison?"

"I think that's one of the best cocks I've seen for a long time," she whispered. Abruptly Sarah stopped stroking it and stood up.

"Then you'd better see it really doing its job," she said, undoing the tiny mother-of-pearl buttons of her blouse. The silky fabric fell open, revealing a black lace deep-plunging bra. She moved her fingers to the front and pressed between her breasts. It was a front-fastening bra and it opened immediately so that her full breasts tumbled forward. With both hands she began to stroke them gently, her eyes never leaving Alison's face.

"Do you like my breasts, Alison?" she asked. "Max does, don't you, Max?"

Max nodded and sat up on the seat, reaching both hands from behind her and beginning to stroke the hardened nipples. Alison stared as they grew even harder, and watched as Max began to squeeze them gently between his fingers, pulling them until they stood out like organ-stops, dark rose against her white skin. She began to moan as pleasure mingled with the pain of his squeezing fingers.

Sarah moved her hands down to her hips and slid her skirt up above her hips to her waist. Alison stared. She wasn't wearing any panties—just a black suspender belt and sheer lacy-top black stockings. Her mound of blonde pubic hair was neatly trimmed, and formed a perfect triangle over her sex. Still facing Alison she raised one leg so that her thighs straddled Max. As she did so Alison caught a glimpse of her crimson slit, wet as her own, now that she was moments away from sex.

"Touch me, Max," she ordered, still looking at Alison. Max's fingers appeared between Sarah's legs and began to rub up and down the slit, parting the labia and hesitating on the little crimson pearl at the top. "Yes—that's right," she whispered. "Just there, Max—you've found it. You always find it." She sighed as the fingers pressed harder and Alison leaned forward so that her face was no more than a foot away from Sarah's moist cunt. Then without warning Sarah sat down abruptly on Max's cock, plunging it deeply inside her with a strangled cry of pleasure.

"You're so big, Max!" she cried. "Give it to me! Give it to me hard!"

Max jerked his hips up and down and Alison, unable to resist, kneeled on the floor of the compartment, easing herself between Max's knees until her face was an inch away from Sarah's vagina. She stared in fascination as the long shaft slid in and out of her cunt, which pulled the skin so that it seemed to grasp the glistening penis like a rubber glove. She heard the sucking noise it made and she smelled the musky odor of Sarah's cunt, and her senses reeled.

"Show me your cunt," gasped Max to Alison, moving his head slightly to the side so that he could get a better view of the girl on the floor. "Open your legs wide and let me see it while I'm fucking Sarah."

Alison slid her skirt up to her waist and pulled down the ivory lace panties that she was wearing, easing them over her knees and sitting back to remove them completely. She opened her legs and Max gasped.

"Give them to me," ordered Max, pointing to the panties that she held in her hand, and she handed them over, her eyes still fixed on the thrusting penis as it slithered in and out of Sarah like a snake. He took them in his right hand and pressed them to his nostrils.

"Mm! Delicious," he whispered. "You'd love these, Sarah. Here, smell them." He passed them to Sarah, who held them to her nose and inhaled deeply before beginning to bounce up and down even more frantically. Her breasts danced wildly and the nipples had grown enormous. Tentatively Alison held out a finger and began to stroke them. She had never touched a woman's breasts before and it felt strange—unusual but erotic. She could imagine exactly what Sarah was feeling as she tweaked the ends of the nipples and stroked the firm orbs in exactly the way that she loved having her own breasts stroked.

"Oh, yes, Alison. That's wonderful," breathed Sarah.

Then Alison moved her finger down toward the thrusting cock and she began to stroke the shaft as it slid in and out of Sarah's cunt. It was slippery with her juices and she encircled it with her fingers, feeling the hot, fleshy folds of Sarah's labia press against them each time her buttocks rammed against the base of the cock.

"Touch my clit," ordered Sarah, and Alison released the cock. She parted the labia and felt around. She had never touched a woman's clit before, though she knew exactly where to find it. The crimson pearl swelled under her fingers and she pressed hard. Sarah began to move frantically on the cock and her breathing became more and more rapid as she started to orgasm.

"That's it! Hard! Both of you! Hard. Yes! YES!"

A moment later she collapsed on Max's knees, leaning forward so that her hair brushed Alison's face. "Oh god," she moaned. "That was fantastic."

She rose and the cock slid out of her. Alison stared at it in fascination, noticing that it was still rock hard. How she wanted it! She sat on the floor between Max's legs and began to slide her fingers in and out of her own slippery vagina. Sarah moved behind her and kneeled down, wrapping her arms around her and moving her hands over her breasts. Slowly she began to undo the buttons of Alison's blouse, and as Max watched she slipped it over her shoulders and undid the ivory lace bra at the back. Then, when her full breasts were exposed, she began to knead at the skin, pulling at the nipples the way Max had pulled at hers earlier. Alison moaned with pleasure and her fingers delved further into her own cunt. She had masturbated many times before but this was more intense than anything that she had ever daydreamed about.

"Lie back," ordered Max, slipping his shoes, socks, and trousers off and kneeling on the floor of the compartment. Sarah moved back and rested her back against the seat, opening her legs wide and allowing Alison to slide against her, so that she lay with her back resting against Sarah's belly. At the base of her spine she felt Sarah's pubic hair tickling her lower back and she shivered. Still the long fingers caressed her breasts and Alison opened her legs wide again to let Max see her sex properly.

"Gorgeous cunt! It's so beautiful. So wet and swollen," he breathed.

"Lick it," said Sarah. "Let me watch you lick her cunt." Alison moaned and strained her hips toward Max's face. He bent down and began to lick the slit from top to bottom in long, slow moves, his tongue teasing the clit before snaking down to the opening of her vagina.

"Now kiss me!" cried Sarah. "I want to taste her on your mouth. Give me your tongue—now!" Max raised his head and moved his face toward Sarah's, his tongue out and wet with Alison's juices. He plunged it into Sarah's mouth and she sucked it greedily.

"It tastes delicious," she said. "Give me more."

"Come and get it yourself," suggested Max, and Sarah eased herself out from behind Alison's trembling body. She moved round to face her and bent her head to suck Max's cock for a moment.

"I want to compare your taste to mine," she murmured before lying flat on the floor, level with Alison's soaking cunt. Her tongue flicked between the folds of skin and she began to caress the dark curly hair with the tip of her finger, moving it sensually around the clit in time with her probing tongue. Then she found the pearl with her tongue and she pressed her face hard against it, sucking hard and nibbling gently with her tongue. Max slid his fingers below Sarah's wet lips and found Alison's cunt. He plunged in deeply, first one finger, then two. Then three fingers were moving in and out of her at the same time as the tongue and lips were working their magic on her clit.

"I'm coming!" gasped Alison. "I'm almost there!"

"Not so fast," said Max, moving Sarah's head to one side. "Kneel on all fours—and Sarah, sit on the seat."

Alison knelt down with her back to Max and watched as Sarah sat down on the seat in front of her and opened her legs wide. The slit was even more swollen than it had been when Max had fucked her, and the juices of her come glistened between the folds of her labia.

"Lick her whilst I fuck you," said Max. "I want to see you do that when I come."

Alison wanted Max's cock inside her so badly that she would have done anything he asked at that moment. With a groan she plunged her face into the wet cunt and began to suck at the crimson bud that had swollen to almost an inch now.

She tasted wonderful, slightly salty, like a juicy treat but much better. Greedily she sucked, relishing the moisture that was oozing into her mouth. Then she felt Max's cock enter her vagina and she gasped. She had wanted this since the first moment she set eyes on him—and taking it inside her whilst her lips were round another woman's cunt was more exciting than anything she had ever done in her life before.

Harder and harder he thrust, and with each thrust Alison sucked more greedily at Sarah's clit.

"I'm coming—NOW!" she screamed, lifting her lips from Sarah's slit. Then Max groaned and Alison felt him stiffen. A moment later she felt his come flood her cunt, then his cock twitched a few times before he slid out of her with a sigh.

"Don't stop!" cried Sarah. "I'm almost there! Lick me again! Suck me!" Alison bent forward and began to suck again until finally Sarah screamed, "NOW!" and she sat back against the seat with a sigh. For a long moment all three sat, exhausted, staring at each other in amazement.

"That was the best sex I've ever had in my life," breathed Alison. "I've never known anything like it before—it was wonderful." Sarah smiled.

"You should make this journey more often, darling," she murmured. "You'd be surprised how ready most people are to indulge themselves in a bit of fun on long journeys. There's nothing like the prospect of boredom to make people behave a little 'out of character.' Take you, for instance. I bet you never thought that you'd end up doing what you just did on this trip?" Alison smiled and shook her head.

"I nearly came to Edinburgh last year. Now I wish I had!"

"Well—now that you know the ropes I'm sure that this will be the start of many pleasant journeys to come."

"I'll certainly never forget this one," said Alison. "And I don't think there will ever be a better one either!"

"You never know, darling," said Sarah. "Strange things happen when you least expect them."

As they dressed, the sliding door opened and a tall, fair-haired man in a uniform entered.

"Can I see your tickets, please?" he asked, his eyes travelling down to Alison's cleavage, which was visible between the folds of her blouse that she hadn't yet fastened. Then he looked up and his face broke into a welcoming smile.

"Hello, Steve!" Max and Sarah welcomed the ticket collector like an old friend. They shook hands warmly and made the usual comments about how well each of them looked.

Then Steve turned to Alison and said to Max, "Aren't you going to introduce me to your friend?"

"I'm Alison," she said, lowering her eyes shyly. If Steve knew Max and Sarah so well, then he must know what she had just been doing with them, she decided. Not that she was ashamed of it—just that she found it a bit embarrassing. But Steve was looking at her now with anything but embarrassment filling his eyes.

"They certainly know how to pick them," he said appreciatively. "You've got a beautiful body Alison." His eyes smouldered and a shiver of anticipation ran up Alison's spine.

"You should see it in the flesh," said Max, and Steve grinned.

"I intend to—later. After we've stopped at York, how about letting me join you for a bit of fun? Have you ever had a foursome, Alison?"

Alison shook her head.

"No—but I'm game for anything after this morning."

"Good. See you all in an hour, then," said Steve with a grin that stretched from ear to ear. Alison sat down on the seat and closed her eyes. This had truly been a wonderful journey so far. Two lovers in the space of two hours! And as she fell into an exhausted sleep her dreams were full of Max, Sarah, and Steve.

Steve!

Boyish and handsome, with a cheeky grin and a long, lean body. Five minutes ago she wouldn't have believed it possible—but now she really believed that the last leg of the journey might even be more enjoyable that the first.

WHEN I MAKE YOU SAY NO

Julia Price

I've got this fantasy that sometimes kind of freaks me out. I have it a lot.

It doesn't freak me out to be submissive; that's no big deal, now and then. It doesn't freak me out to be sexually dominant, either—I do that a whole lot. But what freaks me out about this fantasy is that it's very important that I suck your cock—and you, fighting all the pleasure pulsing through your body, say "No."

It doesn't matter if you're older or younger, big or small, thick or thin, black or white. What matters is that you're a really tough, alpha-male type (maybe even a little bit of a sexist pig) who loves it when I go down on you, and still I make you say "No."

In this fantasy maybe we're already fooling around, or maybe we're just watching TV on the couch and I slide down onto my knees and start to unzip your pants. You get this cocky smile on your face. You know what's up; you know you're about to get a blow job. It makes me wet to know you know. It makes me wet to see that sense of entitlement on your face, that sense of satisfaction. You don't say "No" yet. On the contrary, you're pleased as punch that I'm going to suck you off. You're pleased as punch that your cock turns me on—you know it does.

I get your pants open and take your cock in my mouth. I swirl my tongue around the head and slide my lips down the shaft until it touches the back of my throat. I let it rest there a long time, sucking gently, my tongue surging and throbbing against the underside of your cock. I come back up for air and pay the head some more attention. I lavish affection on it, glancing up every now and then to see you watching me, cocky smile still on your face. It makes me mad and wet, at the same time, to see how self-satisfied you are. To see how pleased you are that I want to suck your cock, that I do it without being asked.

Maybe you've already got your shoes off; I reach behind you and slip my hands down your pants—jeans, let's say, oil-stained jeans, smelling of diesel and sweat and musk. You lift your ass in the air so I can pull your smelly jeans down to your ankles, then over your feet. Your underwear, it goes without saying, comes with the jeans. You sweep your black T-shirt, let's say, over your head, toss it on the floor.

Maybe you've got muscles and a finely chiseled physique; maybe not. Maybe you've got some tattoos, something butch, a Harley or something like that. I go back to pleasuring you, my lips gliding over your shaft and my tongue working hungrily back and forth. Then I take you in my mouth and suck you some more. When I look up at you, you're cockier than ever, but your face is turning red as you flush with physical pleasure. The mental and emotional pleasure peaked the moment I took your cock in my mouth. It'll peak again if I swallow your come, which I fully intend to do.

But like I said, before I do that I'm going to make you say "No," and mean it.

Maybe at this point you hit a button on the TV remote. Maybe you flip from TV to DVD, maybe you hit PLAY. Start watching a porn movie. I don't even turn my head to see what you're watching; I already know. Something filthy. Something with lots of anal, rough, as dirty as it gets. Something that makes your cock even harder in my mouth, makes you moan softly as I go down on you. You get more and more turned on, and I know if I wanted to I could make you come easily. There's an intense sense of power in that, knowing that all it takes is a little head to satisfy you. But it takes a lot more to satisfy me, and in my fantasy I'm going to get it, no matter what.

As my head bobs up and down in your lap. I wriggle my hand down behind your balls. I gently tickle them, which makes you moan louder. Your balls are tight and firm against my fingertips; I can tell you're ready to go; just a few of the right kind of thrusts, and you'd fill my mouth with your come. Did I mention I don't swallow in real life? Doesn't matter; I'm going to swallow in my fantasy. Right after I make you say "No" enough times.

I grab your balls and pull them down, gently at first, then more firmly. Your moans turn into a stifled whimper of surprise, but you let me do it. Your orgasm recedes as I circle my fingertips around your balls. I squeeze them softly at first, then harder, feeling you squirm as I do. I look up at your face and it turns me on to see confusion there. You're not sure how to respond. You love the feel of my mouth sliding up and down on you, of your cock being deep inside me, the head pressing against my throat. But the way I'm squeezing your balls makes them ache a little bit—just a little bit—and you're not sure you like that. You say "Hey!" but then I take your cock deep, nuzzling the head into my throat, swallowing, and your protest turns into a long, low moan of pleasure as I tug on your balls harder. You writhe on the sofa, maybe let your hands rest on the top of my head—lightly, not yet grabbing my hair—and feel me bobbing up and down on you. I pull harder and you whimper helplessly, tangled in my web of pleasure and pain. I squeeze more firmly and you gasp, then settle into a long sigh.

Maybe you say something at this point. "Don't squeeze so hard," perhaps. Maybe you even say "Please." Or maybe you don't. Your voice might be helpless and desperate, pleading, whining, or it might be dominant, as if you're telling me, not asking me.

I respond by pulling harder, and you lose it, groaning and arching your back on the couch—but not pushing me away. Yet. I swallow your cock in deep thrusts, coming up to suck and lick on the head now and then. You're done protesting for the moment; when I squeeze your balls you just thrash, your fingertips on the top of my head, ready to push me away the instant the pain and the pleasure reach the wrong combination. But when I look up at your face, you're lost in conflicting impulses—you don't know what to do. Maybe you like having your balls squeezed, just a little. Or maybe a lot. The important thing is that you don't even know yourself, or can't admit it to yourself. With my mouth and my hand, I've blown your fucking mind.

Which is why I take it to the next level.

Maybe I've stashed some lube next to the couch. Then again, maybe not; maybe I just lick my finger a little and get it barely wet, barely at all, with my spit. Just to ease the passage a little. My hand goes down behind your balls, and you breathe a sigh of relief; no longer will you have to wrestle with that intense pleasure and that powerful ache.

But I'm not done with you yet—of course. Because you haven't said "No." You protested, sure. But I need to hear that word, spoken in horrified abandon, spoken at the moment of your orgasm, when you come in my mouth.

I slide my finger down behind your balls, touching your asshole.

"Hey," you say, your voice hoarse now from moaning. You twist and squirm back and forth, your hands coming down to the top of my head, to push me off you or pull me on—I don't know, and you don't know. I feel your asshole, tiny and tight, puckered and vulnerable. Your eyes go wide as I apply pressure. Your fingers tangle in my hair but you can't bring yourself to push me away. Maybe you even edge down in the sofa a little, getting yourself closer to me.

You're very close, now, ready to come in my mouth. Your balls are tight again against the back of my hand, up close to your cock. That makes it easier to get the proper angle.

I penetrate you with my finger—in quickly, before you even realize what's happening. Your ass is tight around my finger, not wanting to give itself up. I press in harder, until I'm buried up to the hilt, my middle finger deep inside you. I'm sucking you hungrily as I do it, your cock in my mouth and my eyes turned up to watch you. Your eyes roll back in your head. You moan wildly. I know you're going to come harder than you've ever come before, and that turns me on so much that I start to come myself—since, when I'm having this fantasy, I'm always rubbing myself crazily, dreaming of the word you say as you start to climax.

"No!" you gasp, and then you can't say anything, because you're too busy moaning, a great shuddering mix of pleasure and protest, and the come that you're shooting into my mouth is as sweet as can be. I can feel the spasms of your ass as I violate it. I wriggle my finger around and your orgasm heightens, the contractions become stronger as you come harder with each movement of my finger. You tremble all over, your moans becoming whimpers as you finish coming in my mouth.

I savor every drop—the succulent milk of my sexual malfeasance. When you're finished coming, and your cock is shrinking in my mouth, I slide my finger out and climb back onto the couch, alongside you.

I can see the shock, even the shame, in your face. My mouth is still filled with your come. You realize it as I move in to kiss you. You recoil slightly. I grab you, my fingers firmly grasping you under the jawline, and you open your mouth obediently to receive my come-filled kiss. You even swallow as I let your own come trickle into your mouth. I know, because I can feel your muscles moving against my hand. You swallow your own come, maybe because I've shown you who's boss. Or maybe because this is what you've wanted all along.

Sometimes, when I'm having this fantasy, I come a second time as your throat muscles work under my imaginary hand, as I make you swallow your own come. But it's that moment, when you say that tender, terrified word—at the moment you're coming in my mouth—that is always the peak of the fantasy. You're my bitch, and you know it.

I have plenty of fantasies of what I do to you after that. But you never say "No." After I've done you like that, you never, ever, ever say no to me. But I say it plenty of times to you—and every single time, it's magic.

CRAZY FROM THE HEAT

Zoe Bishop

My roommate and I were sunbathing at Baker Beach in San Francisco when it happened. Vanessa is my roommate and best friend. And...I'm not sure what else. But after what happened at Baker Beach, I'm starting to get a pretty good idea.

Baker is an interesting place. If you've ever lived in the Bay Area, you've probably heard of it—even though it's technically not a nude beach, nudity is "tolerated," which means some people get naked and others don't. Of course, most of the time in San Francisco you don't *want* to be nude, because it's foggy and cold as often as not.

But this was one of those rare summer days when the mercury hits a hundred degrees in the city, and everybody in town, so unaccustomed to that kind of heat, goes crazy and strips down to their skivvies. My friend Vanessa and I decided to hit the beach, and found a crowded strip of sand with pasty-white, oiled-up bodies sprawled everywhere. I guess because of Baker's reputation as a gay beach, there wasn't a kid in sight—no screeching brats howling about sand in their swimsuits, no daddies throwing beach balls; just the other kind of daddy, the fortyish guy who brings another guy my age. And even they looked at us.

Vanessa and I weren't pasty-white at all. We had been planning a trip to Southern Cal, so we had already been visiting the tanning booth. For the first time in my life I had a rich, sexy, golden-brown tan, and as Vanessa and I laid out our beach blanket and stripped out of our shorts and tank tops, I felt a glow of pride at my firm and tanned body. I also felt a little embarrassed; this was the first time I'd worn my new string bikini in public, and I could feel the eyes of all the male beachgoers roving over me. It was amazing to me how blatantly the guys on the beach looked at us, not even trying to disguise their admiration, their attraction, their hunger. It felt good to be looked at like that. Even though it made me a little nervous, I liked it.

But what was strange was that there was a line of guys up on the cliffs overlooking the beach, peering down at the beach with binoculars, camcorders, and digital cameras. They were far enough away that I couldn't be absolutely sure, but I felt confident that Vanessa and I were the focus of many of those instruments and the rapt attention of the dirty old men up there looking at us.

The back of Vanessa's bikini was nothing more than a string, but that wasn't enough for her. As soon as she sat on the blanket, she started unfastening her bikini top.

I looked at her with my eyes wide. "Van-*nessa!*" I said, shocked.

"What?" she answered, shrugging as she slipped off her bikini top and tucked it in her beach bag. Her breasts glistened, sweaty and tawny, in the sun. "It's a nude beach."

Vanessa has great tits. Like me, she didn't have the faintest hint of tan lines. Thank God for technology. "But all those guys are watching."

She smiled. "Let 'em look. It's not like they'd dare touch. I've got my pepper spray." That made me laugh.

"They've got cameras," I said. "You'll probably be on the Web by tonight."

"Guess I'll have to give up my career in public office." Vanessa upended the bottle of sunscreen and smeared a handful over her breasts, paying special attention to the nipples. I tried not to watch too closely, but something kind of intrigued me about the way she rubbed the oil all over her nipples, making them swell until they were glistening and hard. How the hell did a girl get so shameless? Vanessa had always been like this, much more daring than me. I glanced up toward the ridge; many of those cameras and binoculars were now quite clearly focused on Vanessa.

I loved that Vanessa was so edgy, but I didn't follow her lead. I brushed suntan lotion over my body, smearing my belly, my legs, my cleavage. Vanessa looked at me and smirked.

"Tit for tat," she said. "Come on, let's see 'em."

"What are you talking about? I'm not taking off my top."

"You take off your top or I'm going to take off my bottom."

I laughed. "Go ahead."

Without a moment's hesitation, Vanessa slipped her thumbs under the waist of her bikini bottom and began to tug it down, squirming as she lifted her ass off the blanket.

"Stop!" I said, glancing toward the ridge. "Everyone's watching."

"Your tits or my bush," laughed Vanessa. "Flash or gash, Zoe."

Vanessa loves to push me like this; she kids me about being

too conservative. She'd even talked me into "practicing" our makeout skills with each other, which had quickly turned into something I wasn't quite sure if I should like as much as I did. I knew I definitely wasn't bisexual, but Vanessa and I did things it still made me wet to think about. And whenever I saw her body revealed like this, I remembered them vividly, wondering if we were going to try them again.

"This hot weather has made you crazy," I said nastily.

"It always does. All right, Zoe, I'm taking it off on three," smiled Vanessa. "It's snatch and patch, or tits and nips. One, two—"

"All right, all right!" I snapped. I unhitched my top and peeled it away from my tanned breasts, trying to hide the fact that my hands were shaking. I felt a weird rush of adrenaline as I exposed my tits, and I couldn't keep myself from crossing my arms across my chest, hiding them from the shameless onlookers.

Vanessa made a "no-no-no" gesture with her index finger. "That's cheating."

"All right," I said, putting down my arms. The second I revealed my tits to the guys on the ridge, the guys playing Frisbee on the beach, the guys doing nothing but lying there on their beach towels looking at us, I felt a flush of excitement. I couldn't believe I was doing this.

"Here," said Vanessa, tipping the bottle of lotion. "We don't want those pretty things getting sunburned."

I blushed deeper than my tan as Vanessa poured sunscreen onto my tits and began to rub it in. I felt her palms stroking my nipples and got even more embarrassed. I remembered how it felt when she'd done that with her mouth plastered to mine, her tongue exploring, and her thigh tucked between my legs, rubbing against my clit through my jeans. I remembered what it had felt like when I'd come, moaning against Vanessa's parted lips.

I don't know why I did it. As Vanessa stroked sunscreen onto my tits—plainly taking more time and care with them than she needed to—I bent forward and kissed her. On the lips. Not a quick one, either. It was the first time I'd kissed her; she'd always kissed me. I made up for lost time, though; my tongue eased into Vanessa's mouth and teased hers as she caressed my tits more firmly, the sunscreen forming a slick, greasy lubricant that made my nipples tingle.

When my mouth left hers, I was breathing hard. My thighs were pressed tightly together, because I was afraid the guys on the ridge could somehow see the heat building between them. Did they have infrared cameras? I was sure my pussy would show up as a blazing-hot sun, ignited by the feel of Vanessa's fingers on my breasts.

Vanessa smiled. "Now they're *really* watching."

And they were. Guys all over the beach were pausing to look at us. When I glanced up toward the ridge, I was damn sure that every lens was focused on us. We would be all over the "beachfront lezzies" website by tomorrow.

"Maybe I don't care," I said.

"Oh, you do," smiled Vanessa, leaning closer to me. "That's what makes it so hot."

She squirted more sunscreen onto her breasts and kissed me. "Rub it in," she said, even though she'd already done an admirable job of oiling herself up. I hesitated, blushing even hotter than the merciless sun was making me, but when our lips touched and her tongue grazed mine, I couldn't say no to her. I pressed my legs together very, very tightly, instinctively thinking I could hide the blazing heat from the imaginary infrared cameras studying us and recording our every move. I put my hands gingerly on Vanessa's tits and began to smear lotion everywhere as we kissed.

My clit felt like it was throbbing. I wanted Vanessa down there, the way she'd been when we were "practicing," when she showed me how it felt to get finger-fucked. I had come so hard I was afraid someone would call the campus cops. No amount of biting my pillow could muffle the moans as I climaxed on Vanessa's fingers. That had been right after Christmas break, and she hadn't done it since; now we just cuddled occasionally. It had been our last practice session, and I only now was realizing how much I longed for a replay.

"You're a great kisser," said Vanessa, breathing hard when our lips parted. "You're going to make some very lucky guy a wonderful girlfriend."

I kissed her again as I pinched her nipples. I had all but forgotten that we were in public, our kiss being recorded on a dozen sleazoids' webcams. I wanted her and I felt bad about it; this was supposed to be practice, wasn't it? But practice for what?

I glanced around and saw a bunch of guys trying hard not to look like they were looking. The guys on the ridge had no such compunctions.

"Why do guys like to watch girls make out?" I asked nervously.

"They like to watch them do more, too," said Vanessa, her hand forcing its way between my firmly closed thighs.

"Oh, no you don't," I squeaked, aware even as I was saying it that I didn't sound very convincing.

"Oh, come on," she said. "Just a little practice? Some day your boyfriend is going to want to finger-fuck you on a nude beach." Her smile looked wicked, vicious, as if she was in total control of me and she loved it. I let her push my thighs open and felt her fingers trailing up the inside of my sunscreen-greased thigh. I couldn't believe I was doing this. I just couldn't believe it. Her hand slid down the front of my string bikini bottom and I felt her fingers pushing into my Brazilian-waxed crotch. She entered me with two fingers, her hand stretching my bikini as her thumb worked my clit. I opened my mouth to beg her to stop, but I couldn't. I was too close to coming.

All that came out of my mouth were little squeaks and tiny moans of pleasure, as I felt the cameras clicking and whirring away, capturing my ordeal forever. I wanted to tell her "Don't." I wanted to tell her "Stop." But I didn't, because I couldn't, because stopping was the very last thing in the world I wanted her to do. I wanted her to keep fucking me until I came.

I finally managed to whimper out a sentence, though I have no idea why I picked this one to say. "This isn't practice," I said.

"No, it's not," Vanessa said. "No guy'll ever fuck you like this."

I would have thought I could never come in public—the stress and discomfort of it all would prevent me from reaching the peak. But nothing could stop me now. Knowing they were watching turned me on. But what really did it was knowing that the private little games I had shared in my dorm room with Vanessa were now public for everyone to see. I was eternally branding myself as a lezzie.

I buried my face between Vanessa's breasts and moaned wildly as I came. I tried to keep it quiet because all those guys were watching—many of them within earshot—but there wasn't a chance of that. I pressed my mouth, open wide, against Vanessa's tits and tasted sunscreen as my orgasm exploded through me. Vanessa kept fucking me and rubbing my clit until I started to twitch and squirm, too sensitive to receive any more pleasure. And still I lay there spread, letting her do whatever she wanted to me, content to let her use me until she was done.

"Oh, god," I whimpered when she finally eased her fingers out of my pussy. "They're all watching."

"Yes, they are," she said. "We'd better get going, or we're going to have an awful lot of guys coming over wanting to give us their phone numbers."

Vanessa had to help me back into my clothes. I didn't bother with the bikini top, instead slipping my tank top on with nothing underneath, the sticky sunscreen making it mold to every contour of my skin. I put on my flip-flops and followed Vanessa up the beach, painfully aware of every guy looking at me. More than a few of them were smiling.

When we got back to the car, Vanessa grabbed me by the back of my head and kissed me, hard, tenderly. This wasn't practice, either.

"Take me home," I told her.

That night was the first time we spent the whole night in one bed. We didn't get much sleep, though. I still don't know if I should like it as much as I do, but I don't care, because I do. I like it more than anything else in the world. Vanessa and I are going to be roommates next year, too, in an off-campus apartment. And even with one bedroom, we'll have plenty of places where we can "practice," and no one but Vanessa and me can watch.

TEDDY

J. Sinclaire

I am an intelligent woman. I have completed my years of university, obtained my degree, and run my own successful business. I am quite efficient at taking care of myself, and have been for most of my life. Independent since I was seventeen, I have made a point of not depending on people to reach my goals. I do not take shit from anyone.

"So what?" you ask, surely already bored to hear about my pussy power-play. "Yet another strong woman." While never a bad thing, it is not altogether rare anymore in this modern world. Fifty years ago, I may have made the headlines, but now...not so much as a mention, except in the classifieds. And, for all my ball-busting in daily life, that is where I turned to fulfill my guilty pleasure.

I fought for years to ignore these daydreams, these perverse little fantasies. The longer you repress, the bigger the eventual explosion, as my poor, unfortunate ex-husband discovered. He could not wrap his mind around my requests, and we eventually fell apart. How traumatic, disgusting, and kinky a fetish could I possibly have to merit a divorce? Is it water sports? An undying love for feet? Was I really a lesbian?

No. Not as sensational as all that. All I truly want, in the darkest of my nether regions, is to be dominated and fucked like never before. I know it sounds simple, yet it's not. I intimidate all the men I meet before I even have the chance to get them anywhere near my bed. It's not intentional, honestly, and I have tried to tone it down a bit. True, there have been the occasional walking hard-ons who have attempted to pick me up, but their dominant behavior outside the bedroom has forced me to shoot them down almost instantly. I worked too hard for too long to allow a man to try to take over my everyday life. I will *not* be the submissive little wifey at the dinner party. However, when I get home at night, all I want is to be tied up and fucked like a bad little girl.

This is where Cal comes in. I'm hurrying down the steps of my office, flushing at the knowledge that I'm already late to see him, which will certainly provoke some disciplinary measures.

We met through a mutual friend at a party, and while he was a bit intimidated by me, he never showed it. However, my lovely but not always most tactful friend had mentioned to him the ad I had put in the classifieds the week before.

"Dominant SWF seeks male able to put her in her place..." and so on and so forth. I had convinced her it was just a joke, and convinced myself that she believed me. "I just want to see the responses I'll get," I told her, which was partly true. The responses I did receive, however, were mostly appalling. I mean, at least wait until we've fucked before talking down to me.

Getting back to Cal.... And what a beautiful sight he was to behold. He had an almost puppy-dog look to him, innocent and wide-eyed, with an adorable, shaggy haircut to go with it. Not the most intimidating figure by any stretch of the imagination, but certainly attractive. He played the docile, obedient role all night until the party began to thin out. He invited me to his home and, to my surprise, I said yes. I figured I had enough energy to ride him for a bit. We left in separate vehicles, him leading the way back to his apartment.

It didn't take very long, and to my utter surprise, the moment we stepped in his door, he instantly dropped his shy, docile demeanor. He pulled me to him, his lips rough on mine, and wasted no time conveying what he had in mind for the rest of the evening. I spent the first few moments in shock. Had he really just initiated this? That thought, of course, led to the inevitable bit of outraged pride. How dare he attempt this without permission? Until I finally told my brain to shut up and just enjoy the circumstances.

With one hand behind my head, and the other around my waist, he crushed my body against his. I could feel his cock, already hard and insistent against my abdomen. His hand slid to my ass, kneading the muscles while his fingers tightened in my hair. He pulled a bit, till my head was leaning back, and I caught a glimpse of an evil smile before he lowered his lips to my neck. His tongue danced over my skin, whispers of motion sending chills all the way down to my steadily moistening panties. His teeth nipped at my flesh at random, my neck, my shoulders, and down for a brief moment to one nipple before resurfacing up by my ears.

"If you really want me to stop, at any point say...." He paused for a second, considering the options. "Say 'Teddy.' " I turned a bit to eye him curiously, and he shrugged. "Just came to mind."

He restarted his teasing tongue work, and I wanted to tease

him as well. Swiftly, my hand dropped in between us, to the tip of his cock, and I was rewarded with a low moan in my ear before he grasped my hand with his.

"Not until I tell you to," he whispered sternly as he guided my hand behind my back, entwining our fingers together.

I nodded at him, eager to play along for the first time in my life. He released his hold of my hair briefly as he leaned in for a kiss. Or so I thought. Instead, he nipped at my bottom lip, refusing to kiss me, and when I tried to capture his mouth with mine, I was quickly put back in my place as he grasped my hair again. I was trying to be obedient, but you have to understand that this was a new experience for me.

Letting his grip loosen, he moved his hands to my shoulders, then to the top button of my shirt. He tugged on it, which gave easily, letting a larger sliver of my skin show through. He undid the rest slowly, and I honestly wondered how he could be so patient. My shirt fell to the ground with a flutter and I almost moved my arms to cover myself. Instead, I leant against the wall and watched him, waiting for his next move.

He slipped one finger inside the waistband of my skirt and tugged. I moved toward him, not quite sure what he had in mind. He stepped backward, making his way through the hallways and eventually into his bedroom. The room was dim, filled with unfamiliar shadows, but his eyes seemed to radiate light. He pulled me up against him and slid his hands to the zipper of my skirt. Undoing it, he slid it down my thighs, licking in between my breasts and down my stomach as he did so. Leaving it on the ground, he took my hand and helped me step out of it. Just as fluidly, he pushed down on my shoulders to get me on my knees. I knelt before him, shocked at my obedience but obviously motivated by my now-wet pussy. His hands moved to his waistband and I expected him to uncover himself, and was surprisingly hoping he would. Instead, he slid his belt through the loops and free from his pants. He looked at me for a minute.

"Put your hands behind your back. "

They were there before he finished the sentence. He stepped behind me with a grin, obviously content with my compliance. Stooping down on one knee, he bound my hands with his belt, wrapping it around a few times to ensure its security. Once done, he reached over for something on a desk a few feet away, and slipped it over my head. A leather blindfold. Soft but unyielding, it left me completely sightless and even more turned on.

I heard him move in front of me again, his fingers suddenly trailing down my cheek and to my lips. He ran a fingertip over the bottom one, slipping it slowly into my mouth before continuing over the top lip.

"What do you want me to do?"

His question caught me off guard. I was the one bound, and he was asking me what to do?

"I... I don't know."

Silence for a minute. His hand moved away from my lips. Obviously the wrong answer.

"If you don't know, I may as well just go to bed and leave you here."

I almost whimpered aloud.

"No, don't. I want you to do whatever you want to me."

I could see his smirk in my mind, and the sound of his zipper being undone was almost imperceptible. Nonetheless, the moment I heard it I froze.

"And what if I want you to suck on this...."

His cock brushed my lips, velvety smooth but hard as a rock. Just as quickly as it appeared, he pulled away before I could open my mouth.

I struggled for words, not ever before having had to ask for what I wanted.

"I want to suck you off."

His skin rested on my lips again, waiting for my move. Sliding my tongue out, I tasted him, twirling around his dickhead. He was salty, with just a bit of precum moistening my motions. I slipped my lips around him and took him as deep as I could. My tongue massaged the length of his cock as I began to move my head back and forth over him. He was quite large, larger than I was used to, and I could not get him as far in as I had hoped. I decided to make up for it in other ways. Letting him slide out of my mouth, I trailed my tongue down his cock until I reached his ballsac, darting my tongue out to lick it briefly before continuing back up to his head. He inhaled sharply and, encouraged, I repeated my actions.

Alternating between this, and taking him deeply into my mouth, was beginning to bring him to his climax. I could tell by his breathing, and when his hand suddenly grasped my hair and began forcing me onto him faster and faster, I knew he was going to come. Until he finally pulled me off him and there was nothing—just silence and his heavy breathing.

I sat there, unsure of what to do, trying to ignore the throbbing between my legs.

"You did well. But I'm not ready to come yet. I believe I still have to fuck you."

With that statement, he stepped behind me again to remove the belt from my wrists, but didn't touch the blindfold. I heard the rustle of something that sounded suspiciously like a condom wrapper.

"Normally I would leave you tied up and helpless, but you've been good so far, so I figure you deserve to at least hold yourself up while I fuck you."

I simply nodded, trembling with want. He took my hand and lifted me up, crushing me to him as he did so. His tongue teased mine, his cock pressed against my thigh, and I wanted him so bad I didn't know if I could stand any more. Without warning, he turned me around and guided me forward until my knees struck something solid. He pushed down on my back, and I reached blindly until I found the top of the desk. There I rested on my arms, and he kept one hand on the small of my back, his other hand drifting over my thighs and ass.

SMACK! Catching me completely off guard, he had slapped my ass and my body lurched against the desk. My nails tried to dig into the surface as the warmth began to spread over the cheek he had hit. I had never been spanked before, and wasn't even aware it could be erotic until now. His hand rubbed the spot he had just focused on, before he slid one finger over the damp area of my panties. The brief touch to my clit caused me to moan aloud.

SMACK! He hit me again, this time the other cheek, and it seemed that this hit had sent fire straight to my pussy. I wanted to come, I wanted him to fuck me, and I just wanted pleasure more than I ever had before. This time he slipped his finger inside my panties, trailing up and down between my lips as I squirmed underneath him.

"This is what happens when you misbehave." He pulled his hand away to strike me again, just hard enough to sting and make me want more. I bucked against his hand, as his finger slipped inside me for a brief second.

"But you've been good.... So you'll have to settle for this instead."

With one easy move, he pulled my panties aside and slid inside me. He was so huge that for a moment I thought there would be pain. The feeling subsided, though, and replacing it was the realization that he was directly pressing against my G-spot. He slid out a bit, before moving back in and, oh god yes, that *was* my G-spot. I also realized he had somehow managed to slip a condom on in between his teasing.

Everything else fled from my mind as he began a slow, rhythmic pace. Teasing even now, he could tell from my moans that while the pressure felt fantastic, it wasn't enough to make me come. He sped up a bit, his hands gripping onto my hips as the sensations rose in me.

"Do you want me to fuck you harder?" His voice was almost a growl from behind me.

"Yes.... Fuck, yes."

He slammed into me harder and harder, as my orgasm built, almost to the climax, and just when I thought I was going to plateau forever, he slipped his hand between us to rub my clit in small circles. I came harder than I ever had before, my muscles spasming around his cock, and I felt him let go inside me, no doubt triggered by my tightening. I collapsed onto the desk, unable to support my weight any longer. His hands gripped my hips hard, as he rode his orgasm out.

That was our first night. Just when I thought he wouldn't be able to top that, I had seen Cal's place with the lights on. Many of those unfamiliar shadows turned out to be restraints and other goodies, which of course he had used to torment me with for hours. More importantly, he had turned me into a content submissive, something I'd never thought possible. Except, of course, for the occasional slip-ups once in a while.

Such as right now. I turn off my car, already in front of his apartment. Memories had blanked out my entire trip here, but now I have to go in and face the music. Oh, how hard it is to pretend to dread what I have been looking forward to all week. Nonetheless, I wipe the "domineering bitch" look off my face as I step through the door. Innocent façade on, I know he will never fall for it, but the game just isn't as fun without it.

"You're late."

He is standing in the doorway to his bedroom, in low-riding jeans with no shirt. Walking slowly toward him, I accept my fate. And hope it will be just as good as last time.

THE ACCIDENTAL EXHIBITIONIST

Debra Hyde

Goose bumps peppered Cara's skin as she left the warm bathroom for the bedroom of her hotel suite. She dumped her toiletries into their overnight bag and, hands free, she rubbed the chill from her arms. Clothes, she wanted her clothes. She wanted to bundle herself away from the chill and settle into warmth and comfort. That and a warm cup of cocoa would work just fine.

Her lover, however, had different ideas. Michael always did, especially when they traveled to fetish events. Where Cara once found fetish events fun and exhilarating, great for finding erotic amusements and watching people, all that changed when Michael came on her scene. To him, every event was an opportunity to put his dominance front and center, to make obvious the claim, "I own her."

Cara spied the clothing Michael had laid out for her, and she knew this time would be no different. He intended to dress her as eye candy—*his* eye candy. Which meant no leather skirt and corset for her. No playful fantasy fairy wings or teasing schoolgirl uniform. And forget her favorite, the leather-and-Levis attempt to mimic certain hardcore gay men. No, Michael had other ideas, and it involved slutwear.

Slutwear, his favorite. And Cara knew what to expect: a micro-mini, thigh-high stockings, a cleavage-creating top, and dainty little shoes that made her traipse delicately. All told, it exaggerated her femininity, turning it from almost-tomboy to something that was equal parts hooker and porn star. And near the damning evidence stood Michael, clutching a long length of metal chain.

"Come here," he commanded, motioning her to stand before him.

He draped the chain forward from behind her neck, its rings falling over her shoulders in uneven lengths. He clipped the short end of the chain to the longer, just between her breasts, then wrapped the longer length around her waist and ran it between her legs until it ended at her waist. There, he locked its meeting points with a single combination lock. The weight of the metal hung on Cara, effectively harnessing her.

"Dress now," Michael directed.

Cara looked at her wardrobe and stopped short. The requisite push-up bra and scoop-necked top were missing. Instead, a red blouse sat in their place, one so sheer that it was obviously meant to be worn over skimpy camisoles.

But a camisole was nowhere in sight. Cara looked at Michael. He offered no explanation, just a devilish grin, a bit of a chuckle—and two small, round adhesive bandages, one for each nipple. Stuck to her, they were just large enough to meet the letter of the law.

"Go ahead," he urged. "Put the blouse on."

She dressed slowly, hindered by the chain's weighty hug. Each item found its place on her body, but she moved so methodically that it almost dulled her senses. Michael, however, preferred drama and as soon as Cara buttoned up, he grabbed her by the hair and dragged her over to a full-length mirror. He undid two of the buttons of her blouse and spread wide the lapel in a blatantly tawdry gesture.

"I think men will enjoy seeing you like this."

Cara witnessed her reflection. Pale skin exposed, compromised, she was as near to naked as she could ever want to be. Her breasts were completely visible, for the blouse did nothing to obscure them, and the chain and the adhesive bandages only seemed to accentuate them. *Go ahead,* they seemed to say, *look at her. Look at her tits.* But they also claimed something even more dangerous, and they spoke in Michael's voice. They said, *Look at what I can make her do.*

A wave of embarrassment washed over Cara, but even in the midst of her humiliation, she knew that Michael always took control, she always followed, and they both liked it that way. Fetish events, if nothing else, allowed them to make obvious to the rest of the world what they preferred, if only for a short time, in a space limited to people like themselves.

Michael latched a leather collar and cuffs into place on her and locked them, and Cara knew what the sight of her thus presented proclaimed: *My flesh is his. My body is his.* And she knew that everyone would see it as territorially as Michael felt it.

"Put your hair up."

As if the blouse and bandages and the leather collar weren't enough, Cara fumbled through what should have been a quick-and-easy French curl, but she was slowed by the dope-like affects of humiliation and submission. Somehow, they transformed a mundane task into something akin to an impossible quest, but she persevered until every long strand was in place. The result left her breasts all the more visible—and Michael's message all the more unmistakable.

The ballroom was a hub of familiar fetish activity. Vendors offered kinky wares, people had dressed with flair and flourish, and from center stage presenters offered demonstrations on everything from liquid latex to strap-on cocks. Cara had seen it all before, but no matter how often she attended fetish events, she couldn't help but get caught up in its contagious enthusiasm.

Michael's slutwear, however, introduced a whole new twist to this annual enjoyment. To her consternation, Cara discovered that she could tell vanilla men from the kinky kind simply by the way each looked at her. Vanilla men, their staff uniforms and badges aside, glued their gaze to her tits, smiling as if today was their lucky day. By contrast, kinky men didn't even notice her breasts. Their eyes went right to the chain and, straight away, they engaged Michael in a good-natured banter about it and "his property." Vanilla men were furtive in their appreciation, while kinky men openly swaggered, but both kinds embarrassed Cara. Both made her feel like an object to be ogled.

Exposed. Cara felt exposed. The gaze of others unnerved her, even in this safe, encapsulated environment. And, regardless of the context, other people's attention meant one thing: She was naked.

Which Michael knew, as he pulled her this way and that while discussing how he had wound the chain around her body. After one particular inquiry prompted Michael to lift her skirt to the gaze of a gentleman who was a total stranger, he pulled her to him and kissed her feverishly.

"People enjoy you like this," he whispered luridly into her ear. "And I enjoy watching them."

His hand went to her breast and caressed it. Whatever composure Cara had held onto now melted into a slickness that leaked out between her thighs. Michael noticed immediately.

"You're aroused," he declared as he held her close. "I can *smell* that you're aroused."

Cara gulped. God help her if the rest of the world's sense of smell was as keen as Michael's.

It helped that, marginally at least, Cara liked the attention and embarrassment that naked tits and a sheer blouse brought. Yes, she struggled with it and, yes, it made her blush, but when it came right down to it, it tapped into the part of her that liked attention—the part that liked *sexual* attention. In time, it allowed Cara to grow comfortable with her surroundings, but Michael, clever and watchful as always, spotted that measure of ease and upped the ante. He clipped her wrist cuffs together and sent her fetching.

"I want something cold to drink," he demanded.

As she made her way to a concession stand, Cara had to wander through a throng of milling people, her hands before her, pressing her breasts together. She tried to avoid meeting the various gazes that watched her pass, allowing herself only the occasional sympathetic acknowledgment from fellow submissive souls.

"Medium cola, no ice," she ordered. She fumbled to retrieve cash from the tiny purse she carried, then fussed with the change and getting a lid on the cup. She wasn't entirely unpracticed in doing mundane things in bondage, for Michael often had her do things cuffed—undressing him, gathering sex toys and whips, feeding him, even cleaning house. But the public nature of serving him while fettered added a level of struggle and exposure that she wasn't familiar with.

Fetish people watched. Leather or latex, dark fantasy or goth, they concentrated on her at work as intently as vanilla men stared at her tits. They all focused on her bondage, on her movements in bondage, on her most minor of accomplishments, and those who squirmed while they watched were, undoubtedly, bottoms made uncomfortable by her dilemma. One even offered to help.

"Thank you, no," Cara declined. "I'm OK."

She didn't know whether it was more difficult to fall under the scrutiny of the implacable, poked-faced dominant or the squirming submissive, but she was thankful when she made her way back to Michael's side where she could at least symbolically hide in his shadow and pretend the worst was over.

The cold winter air came almost as a relief to Cara, after an entire day in Michael's slutwear. Yes, it chilled her exposed legs, and her nose and cheeks felt absolutely frozen, but a warm jacket covered her breasts and Michael's car was in sight in the parking garage. A few more steps and she'd be home free.

But Michael exacted a price even during those last few steps. He grabbed Cara and forced her up against the car. He pulled her jacket open, swiftly unbuttoned her blouse, then spun her around to face the car. He pushed her forward, pressing her breasts up against the freezing windows of his sedan, then slammed his body against hers, pinning her in place. Cara could feel his stiff cock against the curve of her ass. It warmed her where the frigid chill of car did not. The mixed sensations thrilled her in ways the goose bumps early in the day hadn't.

Michael held Cara there, one hand in her hair, the other searching far lower. He reached between her legs and when his fingers found their mark, he started feeding her cunt such pleasure that it readily seeped.

He moaned in her ear appreciatively, kissed her, then whispered, "What a beautiful slut you are."

He slipped a finger into her waiting hole and as he penetrated her, Cara moaned and closed her eyes. She couldn't believe this scenario, that he was doing this to her, here, in a parking garage. Yet it felt so good that Cara longed to yield to it. When Michael brought his thumb to her clit, she shuddered and gave way.

"You're the eager slut, aren't you? You're ready to come right now, aren't you?"

Cara didn't want to admit that, yes, she could come right there, on the fourth level of a city parking structure.

But she didn't have to. Michael stroked her fast, furiously, his hand determined to tear from her that which she was primed to surrender. Rubbing, circling, squeezing, fingers pumped and penetrated, but mostly they worked the hard knob of Cara's clit until she could stand no more. She tensed against a peak both personal and familiar and there she perched until she fell into the deep spasms of orgasm, crying out at its strength, then panting to the rhythmic throbs that overtook her.

Her orgasm barely subsided, Michael felt his way up her body, his hand roaming until he found a tit. He grasped and kneaded it, leaving Cara with a sense of wetness against her skin.

"Be thankful I can't come as quickly as you do," he spoke in her ear. "Or I would've fucked you right here."

Cara shuddered at the thought.

"But that's OK. I'll just shove my cock up your ass when we get home."

Then he laughed. Cara assumed he laughed because he'd have her yet, but when she opened her eyes, she saw that wasn't the case. Ahead of her, two leathermen stood by their car, watching.

"Nice one," one of them said, complimenting him.

"Yeah," Michael agreed. "She is, isn't she?"

Cara froze, too dumbfounded to react. Michael chuckled and opened the car door for her. He took her by the arm and guided her.

"Come on. Get in."

As she sat, Michael leaned in and buckled her seat belt for her. Stunned, she couldn't believe that others had watched her come. She couldn't accept that they appreciated what they had witnessed and that Michael had enjoyed their voyeurism. His enthusiasm, however, shattered her denial as he slid into the driver's seat.

"That was great. I can't wait for the next fetish event."

Cara clutched her coat close as if to hide from the very idea. But a warm throb from deep inside her, met by an unmistakable warmth between her legs, contradicted her and she knew she could no more escape her own desires than she could Michael's enthusiasm. Embracing the inevitable, she let go of her coat and reached for Michael instead. She kissed him, urgently. She had to. She didn't know how else to say, "Me too," and she had to say it before common sense returned to reclaim her.

JEN AND TIM

Kay Jaybee

The courier handed Jen a soft brown package. She signed his receipt pad and headed into her apartment, tearing open the stiff paper as she flopped down onto her bed. The delivery of an outfit had become an important feature of her nights out with Tim. Jen smiled in anticipation of the night ahead as she held up tonight's uniform. "So," she said to herself, "he's obviously coming straight from work tonight." Quickly slipping it over her immaculate underwear, Jen took a few minutes to put the evening's essentials into her holdall and headed off down the street.

The crowd outside the club was buzzing with an air of expectation. Jen smiled sweetly as she pushed her way to the front. Tim, as she had foreseen, was right at the start of the line. A smiled greeting was all that was possible in the assembled din.

The black doors swung open and the clientele surged in, jostling at first by the cloakroom door, then at the bar, before finally being swept onto the dance floor.

Jen, who had opted to keep her coat and stay sober, acquired two bottles of mineral water, before locating Tim at a table in the far corner. "Well?"

Tim pulled her jacket aside and nodded with satisfaction.

"I'm glad you approve." They swigged from their bottles, watching the decadent behavior of those around them. The crowd had already turned into a groping mass. Nurses were wrapped around sailor boys, policemen were behaving as if they wanted to get arrested, and a bishop was doing something intimate and entirely ungodly to a postal carrier. Jen loved this bit. The undemanding freedom of being felt up by a stranger who, just in that place, could be whoever they wanted to be.

Tim leaned across the table toward her. "I have booked a room."

"Oh?"

"I thought we could skip the dancing tonight. There are other things we could do with our time." Tim lightly touched her arm. The electricity shot through her.

Tim smiled coyly as they picked up their bottles and made their way to the back of the dance floor. The deliberately poor lighting hardly made any impact there at all. A tall, seminaked security guard admitted them into a long corridor that had three doors on each side. He handed them the key to the furthest door on the left and walked away. Jen undid the lock and they went in.

Jen had been attracted to Tim's dark eyes and shy smile from the second she had seen him, but any sort of relationship had seemed impossible to him. She knew different and had begun a campaign to convince him that they would be good together, despite his usual preferences. Not a relationship, not even a friendship really, but sex to die for. Jen had been proved right on more than one occasion.

The room was dominated by a giant bed, around which there were various chairs, cushions, and racks of paddles, whips, and enough restraints to please the choosiest of bondage queens. The light was not bright, nor was it that tacky shade of neon associated with many other such establishments.

As yet neither of them had spoken. Jen looked into Tim's eyes. He was waiting for her. Walking toward him she reached out to his airline pilot's jacket and stroked the soft navy fabric. She took off his cap and placed it on her own head at an angle that complemented her long, perfectly straight pigtails. Then she took his hands and placed them onto the buttons of her coat. He undid them and let it fall to the floor. The tight pale-blue air hostess's outfit he revealed fitted the contours of her body perfectly. Slowly Jen unbuttoned the front of her outfit, then let it slip to the floor.

Jen hesitated for a second to let him take in her beautiful figure encased in a cream basque and hold-ups, before sliding on his jacket. She was careful to leave it open so that her body could still be seen beneath its dark lapels. Next she removed his shoes, socks, and trousers, folded them deliberately neatly, and placed them in the corner of the room. Jen stroked his muscular calves and admired the form of his cock as it pressed hard against his boxers.

Next came his shirt. Jen pulled the slightly creased material off his broad shoulders, placing a kiss lightly on each side of his dark chest as it appeared before her. She placed it with his other clothes, before regarding him critically. Jen knew what she ultimately wanted to do to him.

Dressed in his jacket, Jen began to feel the stirrings of power. All she had to do was put on the final part of her costume and once again she would feel what she imagined it was like to be male, at that moment, for that one purpose. Nevertheless she hesitated. Tonight she would treat him, and herself. She sat him down on the edge of the soft duvet that covered the bed and, in an unusual act of submission, knelt down, pulled his boxers to the floor, and placed his deep brown cock into her mouth. A sigh escaped him as Tim felt the firm lips alternate between clasping him tightly, pushing him forward, and then lightening their hold so that Jen could lick him as if he were an exquisite ice cream cone.

Jen knew he was keeping as still as he could, for the second he made any movement she would stop. She began to move her hands up his long dark legs, until she cupped his balls, cradling them softly. Then, with precision timing, she gently inserted her index finger a short way into the velvety entrance to his arse. Tim shivered and reached out, pulling on her pigtails. Jen withdrew. Whilst on her knees she had formulated a plan for the evening.

Tim had already climbed onto the bed, so sure was he that she would be strapping him to it at any moment. "Where are you going?" she asked in a commanding voice. "Stay still and wait until I say you can move." Jen picked up her discarded air hostess outfit and put it on him. It hardly reached around him, and was ridiculously tight across his chest, but to her he looked magnificent.

Tim stood silently and watched as Jen reached into her bag and pulled out her impressive strap-on, wrapped it around her waist, clicking it into exactly the right spot, before hooking its remote control onto the thin leather belt that held it in place. "I have given you pleasure, I expect you to return the favor." Jen pushed Tim to his knees and watched, fascinated, as he began to deep throat her phallus. It was as if she'd been given a huge testosterone injection. Tim was gobbling at her dick as greedily as if it had belonged to one of the many men he had known.

He glanced at her breasts, which he could just see through the gap in his jacket. He looked at her for permission to touch, she nodded, and his hands kneaded her with all the force of a baker attacking bread.

Jen could feel the conflict rising within her. Her breasts ached for the attention only a mouth could give them, but not now. She had to remain as male for him as she could, although she allowed him to tease them for a little longer before she pushed him away. "Now," she said firmly, "I think a change of routine...."

Tim nodded meekly, fluttering his eyelashes as seductively as a young girl. She took his hand and led him over to a bar stool that stood in the corner of the room. "Bend over it."

Tim was unsure. "It's too narrow."

"Are you questioning my decision?"

Tim hastily bent over the stool. "No."

"Feet off the floor, please." Jen spoke harshly. "Stand on the lower rung and hoist your body over." As she was speaking Jen produced four short lengths of cord from her bag. She smiled at his discomfort, yet he had done as she asked, his stomach precariously pressed against the seat, whilst his feet perched on the rung between two of the legs, and his hands reached down to the other two. Jen's practised hands secured him in place, just tight enough to keep him still, but not so tight as to burn. She stood back to examine her handiwork.

Tim looked incredible. Her outfit had hitched up across his back, revealing a pair of lush buttocks, and his dick was crushed against the edge of the stool's plastic seat. She could feel her juices sticking to the inside of her strap-on. The sight of his prone body was almost enough for her to overload on power. Jen tore her eyes away from her whore and surveyed the rack for a suitable weapon. After all, he hadn't done as he was told straight away, had he? There were crops, whips, and paddles of varying sizes, each of which could, in the right hands, cause as much pain or pleasure as required. To Jen it was as hard as choosing between bars of chocolate in a sweet shop, and all the time Tim was crouched uncomfortably on his stool, waiting.

Jen picked up a black leather-coated paddle and felt its pleasing weight in her right hand. Then she tried a short white cane by swishing it around her legs. She could see that Tim had begun to tremble on the stool, his shoulders and calf muscles twitching involuntarily, and she wondered if he was feeling light-headed, for the blood must have run to his head by now.

She chose the paddle. Tim's head jerked up in pain as the first blow sent a stinging sensation across his left buttock. Jen matched the resulting pink blotch with another on the right cheek. It looked beautiful. She slowly caressed each hot mark with a long, hard kiss, before inflicting the punishment again and again until her captive's cries became moans and his ripe cock began to look agonisingly uncomfortable in its enforced position.

Jen's black dick seemed to have taken on a life of its own as it swaggered in front of her when she stepped around to face Tim. She lifted his head and teased his parched lips with her hard tip. "Want this, do you, madam?"

"Yes, sir. Please, sir." Tim's throat was so dry that the words came out as a whisper.

"You'll have to speak up. What did you say?" Jen was thoroughly enjoying the wait, the expectation of what was to come making it so worthwhile.

"Yes, please, Captain, sir." Tim barked the words like a sergeant major, yet a slight quiver to his voice betrayed every inch of his need.

Jen inclined her head. "Very well, madam." She moved back around the stool and arranged a pile of cushions onto the floor, so that she could stand at the correct height. Then she reached between her legs and scooped up some of her own juices to smear along the length of her thick shaft. Stepping up into position, she took one final moment to examine her handiwork, before jamming herself between his exposed buttocks. Jen almost lost control, so strong was the feeling of domination that powered through her body. She leant as far forward as she could, the pilot's jacket falling open so that her taut breasts brushed across the back of his dress. Jen rested there for a while, feeling the muscular body that was caught beneath her, before beginning a slow, rhythmic pumping against his arse, her hands clawing his hair to keep in position.

The shallowness of Tim's breathing told her all she needed to know as she pressed the trigger on her remote, sending delicious vibrations coursing across her enflamed clit and down through his backside. "Oh, Christ, girl!" Tim cried as she pushed him over the edge. That was all she needed to hear, to make her climax in body-raking shivers as she lay across his bound form.

Jen paused to catch her breath, withdrew, and unfastened her strap-on before facing Tim. He looked like the cat who'd got the cream. Jen smiled at him, taking in the sight of his white come as it ran down his legs and the stool. She undid his hands and legs and helped him to rise slowly, unsteady at first, his firm chest framed by her air hostess uniform.

Jen took a last look, before removing his jacket and placing it carefully onto his pile of clothes. Tim passed Jen her outfit and kissed her cheek. Putting her belongings into her bag, Jen turned to leave. "See you in the morning, Captain," she said.

"Goodnight, Stewardess Harper. Sleep well. It's a long-haul flight to Singapore tomorrow, after all."

DISCIPLINE

Tsaurah Litzky

I woke up with a herd of politicians stampeding through my head. Watching the coverage of Reagan's funeral on TV had driven me to despair and drink. I prefer to do my drinking to celebrate—if only I had turned the TV off before I had knocked down half a bottle of Scotch.

I had to take a hot-and-cold shower and drink three cups of extra strong coffee before I could banish those ponderous politicians from my head. I wanted to replace their dark, somber suits with rainbow colors. I drank a large vodka flavored with orange juice and took three aspirins and finally summoned the discipline to totter over to my computer, where my current writing project is a memoir of my life in the late '80s.

I was working on the chapter about my one-night-stand with the rock star who was so famous that for two years in a row his unique first name was the one most often chosen for newborn baby boys. In my memoir, I call him Mr. Rocker but everyone will recognize him as Cockney Craven, possessor of eleven gold records, often called in the tabloids "The Craven One." I was just describing how this famous rock icon with the triple Prince Albert couldn't come.

We had sucked up enough blow to fly the Utah Boys Choir to Amsterdam. I had orgasmed four times while Cockney was plugging me, but he couldn't seem to let go. His member was now bobbing forlornly, despite its three gold rings, and softening at half-mast.

I crouched above him, cradling it in the palms of my hands, playing him with my fingers like a flute, but to no avail.

Cockney sighed, "That's not going to work, that's not going to do it," he said. "But do you have any high, high heels?"

"Yeah," I said, "I have a pair of six-inch heels—red suede pumps that buckle around the ankle."

"That's just the ticket. Get them," he implored. "Get them and put them on straight away." I fetched them from my closet and sat on the edge of the bed to put them on. He was so eager; he helped me, quickly doing the buckles up.

"This is what I want you to do," he said. "Walk around in front of me, walk back and forth across the room."

I did as he asked but felt self-conscious. I wondered if he would notice, seeing me standing up, how my ass was too big for my body or how much smaller my left tit was than my right. I need not have worried because he said, "You're foxy, so foxy, such a foxy lady. Turn around. Yes, yes, that's right, jolly good. Now," he instructed, "put your hands under your titties, shake 'em, shake 'em, rock and roll, turn around, dance for me."

I started to get into it, gyrating before him, thrusting my box in front of his face. I was starting to work up a sweat when he said, "OK, Gypsy Rose Lee, come on over here. Take a look at this." I paraded closer. His cock had revived, and now it was an upstanding soldier, saluting me proudly. "Fantastic," I said.

"Knew you'd like it," he replied. "Now, lift your leg and put the heel of your shoe in my mouth."

"In your mouth?" I asked, surprised. I had never been with anyone who wanted to suck on my shoe before. "That's right," he said, "in my mouth, fucking A." He grinned at me with the charm that had captivated millions.

He reached out and hooked a couple of wily fingers into my snatch, pulling me toward him. With his other hand he took mine and wrapped it around his now stiff, bulging cock. As he moved his fingers slowly in and out of me, I tried to pull them even deeper inside. He had made me eager and I wanted him to move faster, but he teased me, going even more slowly. Soon Cockney had me writhing with pleasure, then he asked me again, "Put that shoe in my mouth. What are you waiting for?" Now I was happy to oblige. My yoga studies made it easy for me to swing my leg up high, and an instant later my shoe heel was between his lips.

I jerked his mighty member vigorously as he sucked lustily at the heel of my shoe. Just as he was bringing me off for time number five, he came too. He sent a thick arc of creamy white jism shooting across the room to land on top of my pink wicker laundry hamper. Then he hugged me to him, kissing my face and the top of my head. I put my arms around him. We lay quietly. His skin smelled sweet, like milk.

He got up and dressed, then before he left, he showed me that fame had not spoiled him. He was still a thoughtful guy. He got a sponge from the kitchen and carefully wiped the dried come off my laundry hamper. I ended the chapter with the Craven One walking out the door as I admired the sight of his tight ass in his black chino pants.

His ass is still tight after all these years. I recently saw him shimmy around in a music video on TV. He has kept working, doing concerts all over the globe. In the tabloids they still write about him, describing him as a living legend, the Peter Pan of Rock 'n' Roll.

I did see Cockney one more time. I haven't yet decided whether I will include our second meeting in my memoir. It was right after Bush number one won in the 1988 election.

My first poem had gotten published in a little magazine named *Frazzle*. One evening, I was sitting at my kitchen table reading my poem over and over. I loved seeing it in print. The phone rang and when I picked it up, Cockney was on the other end.

"How's the most beautiful bird in New York?" he asked.

"If you think I'm going to fall for that line, you're right," I told him.

He laughed and then he said, "I'm so glad I found you at home, lovey. Listen, I'm holed up at the St. Regis, recording session tomorrow. Why don't you drop over this evening? We will have some bubbly and giggle over old times. How about six p.m.?"

I was delighted that he invited me, and I had always wanted to see what the inside of a room at the St. Regis was like.

"You're on," I told him.

"See you then," he said. "Room 530, and remember, wear those beautiful shoes."

At ten of six, I turned off Fifth Avenue onto Fifty-fifth Street. The purple and gold canopy of the St. Regis loomed just ahead. I tottered along on my six-inch heels. I was wearing my favorite red-sequined, strapless minidress under my fall trench coat. At the last minute, I had typed out a copy of the poem that was in *Frazzle* and tucked it in my purse. I couldn't help nursing the fantasy that if I showed it to Cockney, he would want to make it into a song.

The lobby of the St. Regis had marble floors and so many mirrors it looked like my idea of the palace of Versailles. I saw myself reflected in the mirrors and made myself stand up straight. I pretended I was the beautiful crown princess of Spain coming to visit the prince of England. Perhaps my royalty was not obvious, for the man at the front desk looked at me strangely, and I wondered if he thought I was a hooker.

Cockney answered my knock immediately. "Right on time! You're a feast for the eyes," he said, grabbing me, pulling me close in a big hug, my face pressed into his chest.

He was wearing orange leather pants, no shirt, and his feet were bare. I could hear his heart beating like a happy drum. "Come on inside, Luv," he said, and he led me into a sumptuous living room all done up in white and gold.

"A friend just dropped by," he said. "I'd like you to meet him."

I could not believe my eyes. Reclining on the white satin sofa was the gender-bending stud lovely of the rock world, Ned Delicious. His bright red lipstick matched his jockstrap. He also had on a Harley Davidson T-shirt that said MORE THAN A LEGEND, and combat boots. He stood up courteously and extended a hand. "Hope you don't mind the casual attire," he said. The square mirror on the low marble-topped table in front of the couch was dusted with white powder. A long white straw lay on top of it.

I was taken aback at this surprising situation, but tried to stay calm. Was I being set up for a ménage à trois? The idea of a threesome with two men had always been scary to me. It was not anything I ever wanted to get into. Who would put what where? I didn't want two cocks inside me at once. I was too small. What a terrifying idea, it would rip me in two.

Cockney must have read my mind. "Don't be afraid," he

said. "We're just two blokes too stoned to kipper, who are happy to have your company."

I probably didn't look convinced because Ned chimed right in. "Really, even if I had the energy, I never shag a person I've only just met. I usually wait at least two hours. My friend here says you are as sensible as you are fine. Come, sit down, do a line." He pulled an elegant silver compact from somewhere inside his jockstrap, opened it, and shook a small mound of white powder onto the mirror. As he was parting it into rows with the straw he said, "Cockney tells me you've just started to write poetry. Any luck with publication?"

When I told them about my poem's getting published, they wanted to see it. I was glad I had a copy with me. They pronounced it marvelous, ahead of the curve. Ned asked me for it. He said he wanted to send it to a friend of his who had a literary magazine.

Then Cockney said, "Let me give you a bit of advice, since you are just starting out."

I was honored he wanted to advise me. "Please do," I said.

"The most important thing," he continued, "is to keep on working. Discipline, always discipline, don't get distracted. Discipline—that's the ticket, learn when to say no to yourself, and never forget it."

He picked up the straw, bent his head over the mirror, and snorted up the two long lines.

Soon we were all three of us sitting on the sofa, drifting together through simultaneous time. It seemed I had always been sitting there rubbing shoulders with my illustrious friends. Ned took his compact out again, and then again. We were talking about the rumor that the queen mother was into S/M when I felt a hand on my leg, right above my knee, just below where my dress ended midthigh. The hand belonged to Cockney and

I looked over at him warily. "I thought you were too stoned," I said.

"Your beauty revived me, Luv. I just had to touch you when I observed the grace of your legs. The fine line of your ankles in those alluring shoes drew me like a magnet. Leonardo couldn't have drawn a more irresistible sight."

"I don't think Leonardo drew pictures of high-heeled shoes," I said sharply.

"Please don't get angry," he said. "I mean no harm. Your skin feels so nice, like satin, and what's the harm in friends having a bit of fun together? Now tell me the truth, doesn't my touch feel sweet to you?"

The movement of his fingers did feel good, generating waves of gentle heat down to my ankle and up my thigh. I felt increased warmth between my legs. My little jam pot was heating up, no sense denying it.

"It does feel nice," I had to admit.

"That's a true poet," interjected Ned. "Tell it like it is."

Cockney's fingers were now softly stroking my shin, moving downward. He circled my ankle with his other hand. "I can't stop myself from touching you," he said. "Could you, oh, would you, please permit me to kiss all the way down your leg, to remove those alluring shoes and worship your glorious feet? Oh, please, please, please." The most famous rock 'n' roller of my generation was actually begging me. How could I refuse?

"Sure," I said. I was wearing a pair of red fishnet panty hose to go with my red dress and heels. Craven removed my shoes and peeled off the panty hose quicker than you could say, "Gather ye rosebuds while ye may."

He knelt at my feet and lifted my leg, handling it gently as if it were fashioned from delicate porcelain. He bent his head, kissed the arches of my feet, my ankle. He traced the line of my shinbone with his tongue, started kissing at my knee, big warm kisses that fanned the heat already steaming between my thighs. My clit started to tingle merrily and puff up with increased pleasure. Cockney continued slowly kissing his way up above my knee, his thick curly hair tickled the inside of my legs deliciously, and I found my thighs spreading wider, my hips lifting as I opened my magic gate, offering him my oh-so-eager clit and the center of bliss below.

"I smell a sweet, a tasty little sweet," Cockney said. He sniffed appreciatively.

"How I would like to taste it," he said. "If you would be so gracious...." How cute of him to show me he could be a poet too. I gave him my answer by spreading my thighs even wider and sliding down a bit on the sofa, so that I was sitting right on his gorgeous face.

He reached around and grabbed my hips with his strong fingers, steadying me, then he lost no time tracing his wily tongue up to tease my clit. I was soon so wet that I was afraid my juices would pour out of me, drowning him, but Cockney persevered, moving his skillful tongue down into my love hole, fucking me with it fast and furious. Soon I could hear myself yell out, "Oh, oh, oh," and my cunt puckered up, my cunt lips pulling his tongue deep into my heart of hearts as I came. I was breathing so hard I couldn't speak, but then my breath slowed and I looked down to see Cockney looking up at me, smiling, my cunt juice all over his face. Tenderly, I reached down and wiped his cheek with my hand.

I was so overwhelmed with Cockney's attentions that I had forgotten Ned was with us. He cleared his throat, coughing discreetly, and then he spoke. "Watching you two romping away was such a sexy sight, you got me all excited."

We looked up. His excitement was apparent. The top of his

cock head was peering at us like a small crescent moon, poking out above his jockstrap.

"I have a secret," he said. "I just adore watching, sometimes. I adore watching more than shagging. I'd be in ecstasy if I could watch you two some more and wank myself. Would you be up for a bit more loop-de-loop so I could watch and wank myself? Would that be all right? I'm a very polite wanker. I don't spurt all over the place. I wank right into me hand."

"Fine with me, mate," said Cockney, "but how do you feel?" he asked me. He placed his hand on the inside of my leg, gently stoking. Now it was he who was wiping up my love potions. What lovely guys, so considerate.

I heard a bold, confident voice that I didn't recognize as mine at all say, "Go ahead, knock yourself out."

Ned Delicious pushed down the jockstrap and pulled out his fabled cock. It was medium sized and curved, thickly veined and uncut. I didn't gaze at it for long. Cockney was distracting me; his nimble fingers had climbed up inside my snatch. I was so sated I didn't think I could come again, but he kept at it, teasing me, pleasing me, stroking inside my pussy, pulling my clit. My excitement started to mount once more and then he bent his head down to my legs again, below my knees, below my ankles, and started sucking my toes. No one had ever done this to me before. I discovered that the nerves in my toes were connected right up to my clit, and my body started shaking, in a lovely frenzy, approaching a colossal climax. Cockney's other hand was inside his pants, gripping and pulling his fabulous tool. Ned stood above us with a great grin on his face, wanking away. Our movements were amazingly syncopated. When we all came exactly together, Cockney and I were yelling, gasping, and moaning, while Ned threw his head back and started to yodel.

Then Ned went into the bathroom to wash his hands. When

he came back, we sat together relaxing on the sofa. "I love it, I like it," hummed Cockney. "It's all rock 'n' roll, but wow, am I hungry. Want to go grab some chow?"

I was famished. "I'd love to," I said.

"Ditto," said Ned. "I'm so hungry, I could eat the queen mother."

We dressed and took a cab to the Oyster Bar where we feasted on oysters and champagne. The diners at the other tables kept glancing over at us, perhaps wondering if they were really seeing the two most famous rock 'n' rollers in the world dining with a mysterious woman in a red sequined dress.

Cockney phoned me before he left the country to wish me the best. He urged me to continue writing and stay disciplined. I never heard from him again. However, a few months after our St. Regis romp, I got a letter from the editor of an avant-garde London magazine, enclosing a nice check. She wrote that Ned had showed her my poem and she wanted to publish it.

Thinking about Cockney and Ned and those rock 'n' roll times made me remember how freely we acted back then. If I smiled at a man on the subway, he might get off at my stop, and courteously invite me for coffee. Nowadays no one is smiling on the subway; instead we sit reading newspaper accounts about the continuing casualties of war.

I felt angry and sad. I didn't want to work on my memoir any more, so I got up to make some tea. On my way to the kitchen, I flipped the radio on just in time to get the news. The newscaster was talking about Ronald Reagan's career, how many Americans were lifted up by his economic policies. Maybe yes, maybe no, I thought—who knows?

Suddenly the newscaster interrupted his broadcast to read a special bulletin: *Cockney Craven was found dead, in his hotel room in Melbourne, Australia, while on tour. The cause of death is unknown at this time*. What terrible news. I felt so empty and sad. How weird and awful, just when I was thinking about Cockney. I was so lucky to have known him, to have spent some time with him.

He was such a great guy; I started to think about how his music lifted up so many people, worldwide. I decided to pour a liberal shot of Scotch into my tea. Right now I didn't need discipline. I needed to celebrate Cockney and the lasting grace of rock 'n' roll.

THE POWER OF IMAGINATION

BJ Franklin

This need cannot be denied. My hormones are racing, my clit aches, and pressing my thighs together has made it worse. I would risk much for that first brush of a thumb across my clit, that first squeeze of an aching nipple, those first stirrings of excitement when warm lips hover teasingly over mine. But there are some things I will not risk, so today I have denied it to the limit of my endurance. I sat through lectures and studied dry textbooks in the library, and no one suspected a thing. I even went to a friend's house for dinner. Watched a man slide a furtive hand between his girlfriend's thighs under the table. It was almost my undoing—but still I fought.

Now, at last, I am home, and relishing the moment of surrender. The girl next door has her boyfriend visiting, and the walls are thin. I can hear soft giggles and murmurs of delight; she has told me that he has good hands. It's amazing how much girls tell each other, and men would shudder to know what their girlfriends have let slip. We know what they know.

But more than words reveals a man's prowess in bed. One blush, one secret smile, can speak for itself, and is vividly remembered. Being friends with a man doesn't stop your fantasizing about him.

Like now, for instance. I'm lying face down on the bed, grinding my hips against the firm mattress, the seam in my crotch slowly working inward. Undressing would take far too long. Besides, my hands are already busy elsewhere, one at each breast, playing with my nipples through the soft cotton of my V-neck top. Delicious thrills are already shooting through me.

Of course, they're no longer my hands. They're large, with beautiful long fingers and a smattering of dark hair. My friend Brian's, in fact. He has a girlfriend, a gorgeous brunette with pouty lips, size eight at the most; but this is about fantasy, not reality.

I close my eyes, but can still see clearly. Wavy hair, strong cheekbones, stubborn chin: the boy who sat near me in this morning's lecture. I've no idea what his name is. He's kissing my neck, softly, lovingly, so different from those squeezing fingers on my tits. But both feel so damn good.

Blue eyes are dancing at me, the deep blue of Richard's, my ex. Laughter lines around his eyes crinkled when he smiled, but only for a real smile. I loved those lines, loved knowing that he really did enjoy my quirky sense of humor. They still turn me on, even after two years.

I'm so wet. Moisture is trickling between my thighs, and that seam is now right inside my pussy, rubbing against the swollen nub. But I can't quite get it close enough.

The frustration is unbearable. I have to get these jeans off. I'm on my back, fumbling with the button, yanking the zipper down, just far enough so that my hand can slip inside. Oh god, yes, finally.

Martin's voice echoes in my ears, caressing me with seductive tones. I don't know him well, he's a friend of a friend, but I've often overheard his banter with the boys. He likes girls to kneel when giving head, and he likes to fuck from behind. Both suit me perfectly—but not yet. I need more encouragement first. "Such a greedy cunt you have, princess, so hot and slippery. And I've only used my fingers. Imagine how much better my mouth would be, locked around your clit, sucking and licking until all thought stops. Yes, that excites you, doesn't it? I felt your shudder, can still feel your juices dripping onto my hand. Go on, princess, ask properly. Beg me to ease your craving."

I'm begging, of course I'm begging, the pleading words coming so easily to my silent lips. I'll do anything to feel his long tongue probing inside me, moving closer and closer to its goal. My fingers are working hard and my hips instinctively follow their rhythm. That tongue feels incredible, and my legs are spread wide as I moan and cry out for more.

Martin's deep voice again. "You're so responsive, princess, and so eager to please. But you still haven't earned your orgasm. Show me what a good girl you can be, prove yourself worthy of such a prize."

I know what he wants. It's my fantasy, after all.

I drop to my knees in front of him. With a thought, his clothes are gone, and he spills hard and ready into my waiting hands. His body is that of the gorgeous naked man on my wall poster: broad shoulders, firm thighs, muscles rippling across his chest and down his arms. I drink in the sight while sucking frantically on the swollen head. One hand is wrapped around the shaft, and my other strokes the sensitive area behind his balls. His head falls back and sighs of pleasure fill the room. It's almost time.

He orders me onto all fours, and I shift so that my quivering bottom is pointed directly at him. He loves my bottom. It's one of the rules.

The tip of his penis nestles inside my aching pussy, and I gasp in delight. He circles it around and around, and only when I'm whimpering does he plunge the full length inside me, hard and fast.

"I told you good girls would get rewarded, princess. A few more thrusts and you'll be there. I can feel it—the way you're poised on the brink of ecstasy, just needing that last nudge to push you over. I could come right now, leaving you panting and aching. How frustrating that would be—and how wickedly exciting. You'd go crazy, wouldn't you? You'd do anything I wanted, anything at all, as long as I gave you release from your torment."

I would, but that's not going to happen. It's the words themselves, the feeling of surrender while knowing I'm in total control, that combine to produce that extra push to force me over the shining edge.

Those first spasms drive a moan from his lips, and his rhythm picks up speed. The friction is perfect, and suddenly gets even better as his erection brushes that elusive place. The G-spot, or A-spot, or whatever those magazines call it now. My whole body reacts helplessly, inner muscles tightening around his throbbing cock.

"Aha, what's this? You're a naughty girl to gain so much pleasure from such an indecent act. I can feel the climax building inside you. Let it come, princess, let it come!"

The orgasm roars through me and I collapse on the bed. At last. I am filled with content—soft, sleepy content—and my body is completely relaxed.

For the moment.

AIRPORT SECURITY

Dara Prisamt Murray

"Next," he barked, raised his head, and looked at me, his unsmiling, intense blue-eyed stare making me feel very nervous and uneasy.

"I only have this with me." I put my slim leather purse on the counter between us.

"What? No other carry-ons?" He frowned in disbelief as he looked at the meager contents: wallet, lipstick, cell phone. "You'll have to come with me."

He strode to a door marked SECURITY and beckoned for me to follow. Once we passed through the heavy door that automatically slammed and locked behind us, the din of the bustling airport disappeared and the sharp, clicking sound of my spiked heels resounded through the antiseptic hallway, making me feel uncomfortably conspicuous. All else was silence. His rubber-soled shoes didn't make a sound.

"Right in here, Miss," he directed as he opened an unmarked

metal door and brusquely ushered me inside. "You have to be searched."

"But I told you, all I have is this purse." I held it out to him with a hopeful smile and a shaky hand.

"All the more reason for my suspicion," he lectured. "After all, these are dangerous times and this is an international airport. We frequently do random checks and searches, as a matter of course. Considering what you've exhibited so far, I'd be remiss in my duties if I didn't probe further into this rather questionable situation."

I felt my customary confidence and self-assurance withering under his severe gaze.

"You don't have a problem with being searched, do you?" He gave me a moment to consider and when I said nothing, he went on, "If you have any objections, I can contact my supervisor, or perhaps you'd like me to call in a guard or two?"

"No. No. Please, you don't have to call in anyone. I don't want to cause any trouble," I assured him.

"You realize, Miss, I'm just trying to do my job."

"I understand." I lowered my gaze and could feel his eyes running appraisingly up and down my body.

"Nice shoes." He murmured appreciatively as he stared down at my exposed toes. "Very scanty, aren't they? Not much to them. Of course, I'll have to check them anyway. Can't take any chances these days."

"I can take them off now," I offered. "They're rather hard on the feet."

"But you don't wear shoes like that for comfort, anyway, do you? We both know what those kind of shoes are called," he drawled. "Leave them on for now. I like the way they look on you."

I felt a twinge of fear as I watched him close and lock the door.

"Shall we begin?" He grinned and rubbed his hands together.

"Just you and me? In here?"

"Would you like a stage and an audience?"

"No, but I just...."

"So, what seems to be the problem?" He stepped slowly toward me until he was so close that I could see his black pupils dilating. He rested his hands on my shoulders and I jumped.

"You're very tense," he observed sympathetically as his big hands kneaded my tight muscles, causing my shoulders to drop considerably. "That's it, relax. Nothing to be afraid of. I do this all the time for the ladies."

He was good. My body was definitely relaxing. The massage was so soothing, so calming—that is, until I felt him sliding his fingers under my arms.

"No. Stop. I'm ticklish," I giggled, nervously.

"This is no laughing matter," he warned, tightening his grasp. "Do I have to get one of the matrons to hold you still?"

"No. No matron. I'll cooperate. Please, just give me a moment," I cried as I adjusted to the feeling of his hands firmly gripping me about the ribs.

"That's better," he soothed as he ran his probing hands down to my waist. "I much prefer this one-on-one, don't you?"

"I guess so," I agreed tremulously as I struggled to regain my composure and keep my growing apprehension in check.

As the halting words left my mouth, he stepped even closer to me, so close that I could no longer focus on his face. He glided his hands around me till they came together and then he ran them slowly up and down my back, with each stroke pulling me closer to him, until I could feel him hard up against my stomach.

Nervously, I tried to pull away. I couldn't help myself.

"You haven't anything to hide, have you?" he questioned,

as he tugged me back against his crotch. "I'm asking you a question, girl."

"No, sir," I answered. "It's just that I was getting a bit dizzy."

"Well, you won't have to stand up for much longer," he reassured me. "Besides, I wouldn't let a pretty little thing like you fall."

With that, he pulled me even tighter against his bulge, while at the same time he leaned back from the waist.

"Put your arms around me and hang on tight," he ordered.

I looked at him quizzically and then quickly decided to obey. The commanding look in his eyes was all the persuasion I needed.

"Now lean back."

As I followed his order, he straightened up and I clung onto him for dear life as he reached out with splayed fingers to encompass my breasts.

"You wouldn't *believe* what some women try to smuggle in their bras," he confided, slightly pressing my breasts together.

"Ooh."

"Umm. Nice generous size. They seem to be all you," he observed as he methodically poked and prodded my flesh. "But of course, we can't take any chances. Take your shirt off!"

I looked down and fumbled ineptly with my buttons.

"Now! Stop stalling or you'll really get me angry."

Fingers trembling, I continued to fumble.

"I haven't got all day," he complained, impatiently whisking the unopened blouse over my head and tossing it onto a bare metal chair in the corner of the room.

He palmed the twin mounds of my lace-covered breasts and his slow, sly smile told me that we both could feel my nipples stiffening.

"Very nice," he complimented. "There's nothing in the world like ripe, luscious, natural tits with proud, hard nipples. Umm. Yes, very, very nice, indeed."

"Thank you," I mouthed softly, for I felt he expected me to say something in reply.

"No need to thank me. I thank *you,* Miss." He ran his caressing hands appreciatively and thoroughly around the expanse of ample white flesh overflowing the cups of my demibra, from cleavage to outer curves, then back over the lace-encased portion of my feminine charms.

"Call me old-fashioned, but I like something to hold onto. None of those skinny waif-types for me. Give me a woman with meat on her bones, especially right here." He gave my tender breasts a hard squeeze.

"Ow!"

He frowned at my outburst.

"We have to take this off, too." He delicately pulled on the peaky tips of the bra cups, tugging my tight nipples teasingly through the thin fabric.

"You're in charge," I breathed in resignation. "Whatever you say."

"Stand up straight, let go of my waist, and step back."

I obeyed.

"I knew you'd wind up being cooperative," he said with a broadening smile. "Something about those shoes."

We both looked down, over my rapidly rising and falling bosom, at my strappy stilettos.

"Should I take them off now?" I offered, nervously wiggling my pedicured toes as he watched in rapt attention.

"No. Not now. I already told you what comes off next." He looked at me meaningfully and paused. "Well?"

I must have appeared confused, for suddenly a look of

annoyance crossed his features.

"Your bra, and be quick about it. I don't have time to play games." He tweaked my nipples hard for emphasis.

"Oh yes. I'm sorry, sir," I sighed as I reached back to unhook the fasteners.

"Allow me," he offered gallantly as he let go of my throbbing nipples, reached around me, and expertly undid my bra with one competent hand, in a smooth, suave move obviously perfected with plenty of practice.

He began slowly slipping the satin straps down my shoulders. Instinctively, I pressed my arms against my sides to trap my bra and delay the inevitable baring of my breasts.

"Now you're behaving foolishly again," he chided. "This has got to come off. A visual inspection of the naked breasts is a must."

"A must?" I asked meekly.

"Absolutely!" he declared as he whipped the bra away from me and tossed it on top of the discarded blouse, all the while staring at my vulnerable mounds of pink-peaked, white flesh.

"You do have beautiful breasts, Miss. This is a real pleasure." He cupped them reverently in his hands for a few solemn moments, weighed them thoughtfully, and then gave them a few playful bounces.

Without warning, his demeanor radically changed. It unnerved me completely. Suddenly, he was back to strictly business, and got very severe.

"Hands behind your head," he ordered sternly and let go of my breasts.

Startled, I jumped and colored in embarrassment as my big, unsupported tits jiggled and shook.

"I said, hands behind your head!" he barked.

This time, I obeyed his order.

He reached out and traced my exposed undercurves with slow, deliberate strokes of his fingers, gliding his digits back and forth several times over the same delicate route.

"Surely you can tell that I'm not hiding anything there," I tried to assure him.

"You'd be surprised by some of the things I've seen here," he confided.

"Yes, sir. I'm sure I would," I stammered. "But may I please put my hands down now? I'm a bit uncomfortable."

He raised his eyebrows, gave me a quirky smile, and delivered one more lingering caress, followed by a series of quick squeezes. "No. That's absolutely out of the question. This procedure is not designed with your comfort in mind."

I hung my head, duly chastised.

"I'm employed by the federal government and I'm responsible for the safety of the flying public. I'm an officer of the law."

"Yes, sir. I understand."

"You should be ashamed of yourself," he scolded as he expertly massaged my breasts. "Imagine, a grown woman like yourself..."

"Ooh," I moaned involuntarily as he continued deeply kneading my swelling flesh.

"...acting like a modest little schoolgirl," he continued, giving my nipples a reproving twist, "like a silly little virgin."

He was silent for the longest time, staring into my eyes and pulling alternately on my hard, dark nubs till I couldn't suppress my panting. I just stood there, dazed and trembling, waiting for him to stop, while secretly praying that he wouldn't.

"Well, you're OK. A lot more than OK." He smiled and casually made himself more comfortable in his trousers. "From the waist up, that is. But of course, that's only the first part of the security procedure."

I shivered as I felt his hot breath trail down my body till his mouth was at my crotch. He knelt at my feet and ran his hands searchingly up and down my left leg, then up and down my right, not neglecting my barely covered feet.

"You're wearing stockings. I like that. You're just an old-fashioned girl, aren't you?" He slid a finger into the band of each stocking and teased around my thighs.

"So, that's it then?" I abruptly asked, getting ready to grab my bra and blouse and put them back on. "I can get dressed now, right?"

"Wrong." He smiled broadly up at me, leaning back so as not to be obscured by my outthrust boobs, and suddenly removed his fingers from my stocking elastic, with a shocking, sharp snap to my tender skin.

I winced and shifted awkwardly from one high-heeled foot to the other.

"Now spread!" he ordered as he inserted the flat of his hand under my short skirt, between my thighs, and sawed it back and forth as if to clarify his order.

I stood there, speechless, unmoving, my hands still tightly clenched behind my head.

"Ease your legs apart," he urged, this time softly. "Now, that's a good girl. Keep going. That's it, keep going till I say stop."

He stopped me just before the discomfort became pain.

"Can you stay like that, honey?" he inquired in mock concern as he slid my skirt up over my hips and bunched it around my waist.

"For a while, I can." My halting voice trembled, along with my legs.

"I certainly hope so—for your sake, that is. Spreader bars and manacles give such a bad impression, and they're really an awful lot of work and trouble for me. That puts me in a bad mood. You wouldn't want to see me in a bad mood, would you?" He grabbed my pubis through my panties and squeezed just a bit too hard.

"No, sir. I'll be fine, sir."

"Good girl, that's a very good girl." He pulled my skirt up over my head and threw it to the side.

I shivered, in a heady mixture of embarrassment and anticipation at the rough touch of his hand. I struggled to stay still as he patted his hand lightly around the dampening gusset of my panties as if he was petting a dog.

"Nice fabric. Silk?" he asked, rubbing my mound softly.

"Yes, sir." I tried hard not to moan.

"I like the feel of damp silk so much better than damp cotton," he said, leering leered wickedly, drawing out the word *damp* as if it were more than one syllable.

The knowledge that he could feel just how soaking wet I was, got me even wetter and more embarrassed.

He rested his palm under my puffy vulva and pressed firmly upward. I found myself straining to push down hard onto his hand. He rotated his wrist slightly and made an adjustment, enabling his middle finger to fit right into the widening seam between my lips. He scrutinized my face as he moved his hand back and forth, with each motion, embedding his finger more deeply into me.

Secretly, I wished that there was no barrier, however flimsy, between his steadily probing finger and my hot flesh. I moaned, threw back my head, and began squirming helplessly against his hand.

"Well?" I heard him whisper as he continued his maddening manipulations.

My cunt was pounding. I felt hot, dazed, confused. I didn't

know what he wanted me to say or do. I struggled to control myself and tried to look at him, but I couldn't.

"What are you hiding?" he demanded in a threatening tone.

"I'm not hiding anything, sir," I managed to mumble.

"Then explain to me why you can't look me in the eye." He snapped the words out, still sawing away at my pussy, while kneading my breast with his other hand.

He tugged my nipple hard. I gasped and screwed my eyes shut.

"Oh, yes. You must be hiding something in that sweet little honey pot of yours, otherwise you'd be able to look at me."

"No, sir. It's just that you're...."

"I'm what?" he interrupted angrily. "I'm doing my job—that's what I'm doing. I don't like that attitude of yours."

He pressed my labia tightly together and I forced myself to look into his eyes as he squeezed rhythmically, each squeeze eliciting an answering gasp from me.

"That's it, girl. Look at me. Keep looking right at me." He resumed his excruciating, back-and-forth motions with his finger in my groove.

I fought hard to keep my heavy lids from descending over my glazed eyes.

"Good girl. Now we're ready to go on," he crooned, patting and rubbing my pulsing mound firmly with his palm till I could feel the hood moving steadily up and down over my clit.

"You do realize that these have to come off, don't you?" he asked softly as he removed his hand from my tit and inched it slowly down inside my panties till his fingertip glancingly brushed my little erection, making me, and it, jump.

"I asked you a question, girl," he snarled, pressing my clit to emphasize each syllable as he spat it out.

"Um. Um. I.... I don't remember the, uh, question, sir."

I squirmed and stuttered, struggling to utter the words as he tapped out a menacing code on my sensitive little button.

"Ah, yes," he murmured, so softly it seemed as if it was only to himself. "You must be hiding something."

Abruptly, he stilled his hand.

"But I'm not, sir. I swear, I'm not hiding anything."

He took both his hands from my body.

That did it. Immediately, I began to cry. I *needed* his hands. He'd brought out my hunger. I felt desperate, horny—humiliated. I had to fight the urge to beg him to put me out of my misery, to put his hands down my panties, to keep rubbing and stroking and tapping, to push me to that orgasm that was building up inside me.

My tears seemed to soften him, to make him aware of my growing need and desire to cooperate fully with his stimulating and excruciatingly thorough security procedure.

"Here, let me help you," he offered as he gently inserted his thumbs into the elastic of my sole remaining garment, aside from my shoes and stockings, which he seemed to be saving for last.

I nodded my head and then looked unwaveringly into his eyes as he slowly drew the panties down over my hips, leaving them held in place, stretched by my widely spread thighs. I made no effort to close my legs because I knew that I was supposed to wait for his orders. They would have to remain as they were until he told me what to do.

He backed away from me and I could feel myself blushing all over as he inspected my body thoroughly and carefully, from my breasts and belly, down over the curly dark bush shielding my sex. I wondered if he could see the small drops of liquid that I could feel trickling down the insides of my thighs.

I warily followed him with my eyes as he began slowly circling me. When I could no longer see him, I felt his hot breath inflaming my neck, teasing me between my shoulder blades, then trailing down my spine till his heat burned at the undercurve of my buttocks.

"Spread!" he ordered.

"Spread what?" My voice quavered.

"Those big blushing cheeks of yours."

"But why?"

"Isn't it obvious?"

I realized that his question was rhetorical, so I kept quiet. I didn't want to make him angry.

"You've been pretty cooperative and that's made things easier for me, so I guess I'll be a nice guy and make things easier for you." He stood up, reached around me, and tweaked my nipples. "How's that, girl?"

"Very good, sir. Thank you, sir." I was referring both to his sentiment of concern and, secretly, to his handiwork.

"Tit for tat," he said as he repeated the gesture, this time a bit harder. "Now, bend right over and let me see you pull those wet little panties all the way down...real slowly."

This is making it easier for me? I thought as I hesitated, because my panties were down as far as they could go, considering the position my legs were in.

"You may close your legs for this. Just slip off those silk knickers and then we'll get back to business."

I tried to concentrate on the loud ticks of his watch rather than on the louder sounds of his labored breathing, and my own. Anything to remove me from myself somewhat, while performing such a lewd display for him.

"Stop right there," he instructed brusquely, the moment my fingers brought the small, filmy garment to my ankles. "Step out of them."

I did.

He circled slowly back around until he was standing right in front of me. "Hand them to me."

I obeyed.

"Spread your legs again, just like before, bend over, and look up at me."

I followed those last two orders with some reluctance, for I guessed exactly what I'd see when I looked up. And I was right. My eyes were greeted by the sight of him rubbing my fragrant underwear over his mouth and nose, inhaling deeply and appreciatively.

"Nothing fishy here. Just the scent of a good, healthy cunt," he assured me with a lascivious grin.

I forced myself to keep looking up at him even though I felt mortified and my back and neck were aching. I wanted desperately to straighten up, but I didn't dare. I watched as he took one last lingering whiff and then tossed my panties to where the rest of my clothes lay.

Suddenly, I felt a thick finger slipping into my hungry, wet hole. My eager muscles gripped him spasmodically and automatically. It was now out of my control.

"This is what I meant by making it easier for you." He wiggled his finger around inside me and pushed it in and out a few times, the slurping sound of my churned-up juices making me wince with embarrassment as I moaned with pleasure.

"We don't need all this for lubrication," he commented, "though it would be a real shame to waste it. Don't you agree?"

"Yes, sir," I whispered just before groaning as I felt his digit withdrawing gradually from my tight grip.

I watched him as he licked his finger slowly and with great relish.

"Umm. Delicious," he complimented me, then ran his tongue in exaggerated circles around his lips before smacking them loudly in appreciation.

All I could do was remain bent over, looking up at him, listening to his slurpy, sloppy noises as he made a meal out of my all-too-obvious arousal.

He gave his finger one last long suck and officiously announced, "Back to business now."

He marched around till he was again behind me and then reinserted his finger, easily working up more of my juices. "Now spread those big, beautiful asscheeks for me, girl."

Reluctantly, I complied and waited uneasily for the assault that I knew was imminent. He made me hold that humiliating pose for what seemed like ages. It was so strange and awkward to feel the cool air and his hot breath invading the privacy of my most-hidden place.

I shrieked in surprise when I felt the cool dampness of his lubricated finger teasingly brushing the tender skin around my anus. Reflexively, my cheeks clenched in fear, my asshole tightened.

"You're only going to make this more difficult than it has to be if you don't loosen up and cooperate with the examination." He briskly slapped my bottom with his free hand.

It was incredibly hard to relax while visualizing how my butt flesh was jiggling under his spanking hand and how my shy anal pucker was being brazenly displayed and completely exposed, yet I put my mind to it and really tried.

"That's it, girl, that's the way," he encouraged as he firmly pressed his stiff finger against my back hole. "Relax, baby. Open up. Open up for inspection."

He pressed and pushed increasingly harder until my poor, exhausted sphincter gave up the fight. I felt a strange mixture of discomfort, shame, and desire as he inched his thick intruder up my virgin ass.

"That's it. That's right. Good girl," he chanted in time with the in-and-out motions of his probing finger. "Take it all, baby. Take it all for me."

"Ooh. Ooh," I moaned. "Oh God. Aah," I groaned as his finger forced itself deeper and deeper into my tight canal.

"I guess you're not hiding any contraband up here, but I must say, you certainly seem to be enjoying this very crucial examination. You really are a dirty little slut, aren't you?"

He made firm circles with his finger as he drilled in and out, widening the route with his efforts.

"Ooh. Oh," I moaned. "Uh. Uh. Uh."

"A little harder for Madame, perhaps?" He didn't wait for an answer, but jabbed harder.

He jabbed. I groaned.

"How about another finger?"

He answered my heartfelt cries by squeezing in another one. I grunted and pushed up against his palm as he sawed steadily in and out of me and reached around to tug on my pendant tits.

"You know, there's one last place I have to search," he teased softly as he continued his steady prodding. "Save the best for last, huh?"

His hand left my breast and I heard the sound of a zipper opening and pants dropping to the floor. I felt a thick, rigid cock between my shaking legs. It jerked up and hit my aching cunt hard. I could feel myself dripping onto it.

"Don't straighten up. Get down on all fours."

We moved as one. He sank down to his knees right behind me, his prick between my legs, his fingers wedged in my ass, his other hand squeezing my tit.

"You know, girl, you're getting my dick awfully wet. That's a little rude, isn't it?"

"Sorry, sir," I gasped, as I felt it twitching and bobbing

against me, causing my inner muscles to spasm in sympathy.

"You're dying for the final search, aren't you, slut?" He was teasing me mercilessly.

I could only manage to nod my head between pants and moans.

"You know, I don't have to just use my fingers." He tormented my pussy by running a titillating finger along my gaping slit.

"I know that, sir," I somehow managed to reply.

"Do you know what else I could put in that hot, greedy cunt of yours?"

"Yes, sir."

"Is that what you want?"

"Yes, sir."

"Is that what you need?"

"Yes, sir."

"Is that what you're really here for, girl?"

"Yes, sir. That is what I'm here for. Yes!"

"Then beg me for it," he drawled as he twisted my nipple.

"Please, please!" I cried.

"Please what?" he taunted.

"Please do the final search, sir," I groaned, all pride gone.

"The final search?" he whispered in mock innocence as he achingly-slowly inserted a finger just barely into my cunt.

"Yes, sir. Please!" I was desperate to be fucked. I craved something big and stiff inside me so I could clutch and grind on it. "Please, I'm begging you. Do the final search. It has to be done to me. Please, sir, you've got to do it to me!"

"With what?" he chuckled.

"With your prick!" I gasped. "Just shove your prick into me, now! Please, now! I want it now! I have to have it inside me now!"

"That wasn't so hard, was it? But it's a damn good thing *this* is." He gripped his solid meat and positioned it at the pulsing, voracious mouth of my cunt.

I screamed out in a large measure of relief mixed with a sudden shock of momentary pain as he impaled me completely with one savage thrust of his thick, delicious cock. My ass was full of his fingers, my gripping pussy was stuffed with dick, and with two fingers he beat off my clit as if it were a little phallus. I lowered my upper body and rested on my forearms, so that my hands were free to play with my tits and I was in a good position to buck strongly back at him.

We fucked and fucked like wild, rutting animals. I have no idea how long we banged and slammed hard against each other or how many times I came, or he did. All I do know for sure is that when it was over, we collapsed onto the floor, totally spent, panting and sweating. We lay there for some time, too wiped out to move or even speak.

After a time I became uncomfortable, but I knew that it was not for me to make the first move or utter the first word. I lay compliantly under him, waiting for whatever might come next. It was all in his hands—just as I was.

Abruptly, he rose, quickly pulling up and zipping his pants. I turned my head to look up at him and he gestured for me to stand and face him. He ran strong, possessive hands all over my body, making my breath quicken and my skin tingle with fresh waves of arousal.

"We must do this again, Miss," he intoned solemnly, reaching between my legs and tugging none-too-gently on my bush for emphasis.

I almost gushed enthusiastically back at him that we certainly must, but I was startled into mute submission by his sober, severe expression.

"Same time tomorrow." It was an order, not a request.

"Yes, sir. Same time tomorrow." I nodded obediently and shivered as he squeezed my tits, which seemed to be his way of saying good-bye.

I watched in silence as he strode to the door and opened it wide, without even bothering to check if there was anyone in the hall. He stood in the doorway and turned around to look at me, taking all of me into him, from my stiletto-shod feet, up my stocking-clad legs, over my hairy mound, my rounded white belly, my heavy breasts, my neck, my face, my wild auburn curls. But he saw much more than my nude flesh—he saw my naked lust, my exposed desire, my complete openness and utter submission to him. His total and intimate knowledge of my very being made it impossible for me to meet his gaze. I held my breath, lowered my eyes, and felt a fiery blush spreading over my trembling body.

"And wear those shoes again," he ordered gruffly.

As I heard the door click shut, I let out a deep sigh, licked my smiling lips, and felt my cunt twitch in anticipation.

ENDYMION

A. D. R. Forte

"So...seduce him."

"I can't do that, Will!"

"Why? Because you report directly to him?" Will looked around the canvas and raised a skeptical eyebrow.

"I don't buy it, Ari. You aren't going to let something like that stop you. You're a libertine."

She shook her head, flustered, and Will frowned. "Stay still, please, missy. I'm trying to work here."

"Haven't you seen me naked often enough to know what I look like by now?"

Will grinned and returned to his work.

"Can't ever see too much of a good thing."

Will painted, and she tried to sit still, all the while fuming. What she wanted to do was get up and pace across the studio and kick things. She thought of all her missed opportunities. Nights when Jesse stayed late at the office. Nights when she might have dared to find out whether his appetite matched hers.

How simple it would have been to open his door. Close and lock it after she stepped inside. She could picture him turning from his monitor, faltering in his usual brief, faultlessly polite greeting. He would have given in—forgetting morals and propriety, forgetting consequences in the heat of her arms around his neck, her mouth....

"Arianne!"

Will's voice penetrated her daydream; the millionth such one.

"Sorry. What?"

"I was saying that I'm done for the day. Unless, of course, you want to stay like that. I'm not complaining."

She smiled. The silky fabric draped across her bare thighs moved beguilingly as she swung her feet down from the chair on which they rested, and a spark of pleasant friction traveled up between her legs.

Will had talent aplenty, besides his skills as an artist. And she was mad with unsatisfied desire. She crossed the room and pulled the brushes out of his paint-stained hands, her own hand straying to his zipper and the growing need she felt under her massaging fingers. The paintbrushes clattered on the table and Will groaned as his tongue found and circled hers.

"Jesse's out of his mind if he doesn't want you. I wouldn't care who you were, I'd fuck you."

"Then shut up and do it," she said, and pulled his hips toward hers.

"I have an idea," said Will. She was sitting in his office and it was four o'clock on Thursday afternoon, an hour until the day could reasonably be called over. An hour until they could quit the stuffy world of cubicles and mindless office work for the spring afternoon outside.

She raised her eyebrows. "And that would be...?"

"I'm working on a new piece and I need two models, male and female."

She looked at her coworker for a moment and a slow smile crept across her lips.

"Is this the Selene and Endymion you were talking about for the gallery show?"

Will nodded, his own smile conspiratorial, and then looked up at a knock on the half-open door. She turned and caught her breath, as she invariably did ever since the first time she had seen him. Eyes the color of alpine lakes, and those cheekbones, and that mouth. How many times had she stared at them and dreamed about claiming them for her own purposes?

"Hey. How's everything going?" Jesse said. Always so understated, so nicely professional. God, but she wanted to see this man in the grip of passion, all restraint abandoned to the dictates of his hunger.

"Great. Will's just been telling me about his upcoming show."

He turned that cerulean gaze to Will. "I heard about that. Great job, man! Congratulations."

"Thanks. I'm having problems, though," replied Will with the most tragic expression of frustrated genius he could muster. She had to turn away to hide her smile.

"I've already said I'd volunteer, Will," she put in, picking up the thread and pulling the game along.

"That still leaves me without a male study," he replied, an irritated note creeping into his voice.

She sighed. "You're impossible." Her gaze flickered casually to her boss, the object of her desire, leaning in the doorway.

"Look, Jesse will do it. Right?" She tilted her head back with a half-mocking smile.

"Do what, exactly?" he asked, his tone matching hers. An undercurrent of sarcasm lay behind the words.

They baited each other like this constantly, so subtly as to be completely overlooked by all but the most perceptive, yet nevertheless felt by both of them. And still she did not know whether it meant something, or nothing at all, and he did it simply because she could understand it when others remained oblivious.

"You could be Will's other model for his new painting," Ari said brightly. "You've taken classes on Greek and Roman art, haven't you, Jesse?"

"In college, yes. And that has nothing to do with posing for anything. I think I'll have to pass on this one, Will."

But Will, bless him, had his head tilted to one side, looking Jesse over with a critical eye.

"Actually, you'll do very well," he said with authority. "You're just about Ari's height, so the proportion would be about right. I could really use the help, Jesse."

"See?" she chimed in. "You'll be doing a very charitable thing."

Jesse rolled his eyes at her, and stuck his hands further into the pockets of his loose-fitting jeans.

"I don't think so. You two are insane."

"Oh, come on, don't be such a wuss."

"Yeah. Look, I'd even offer to pay you guys," Will interjected, "but I can't, just yet. And I'd really, really appreciate this."

Jesse was still shaking his head, but she turned to Will.

"Just tell us when to be there. He'll show," she said.

"Saturday, anytime between two and three is good. I'd like to get at least three hours of daylight to work."

"I'm not doing this...."

"He'll be there," she said to Will.

"You ready yet, Ari?"

"Just about," she called back. She stuck a final hairpin into the loose twist of hair atop her head and surveyed the effect. Not period correct, but it looked close enough for Will to get the right effect. And close enough to be becoming for the eyes of her fellow model. She smiled at her reflection in the mirror, and wondered if Will had told him yet that this was to be a nude study.

Evidently not. She walked out of the bathroom in slippers and nothing else, and felt the gaze of both men turn her way—one cool and appreciative, one hot with shock and unspoken lust. Color stained Jesse's cheeks, but his expression remained unchanged as he lifted his eyebrows and turned to Will.

"Please tell me we're covering up somewhat."

Will looked away from her, and at Jesse with an expression of perfectly innocent surprise.

"Oh, no. This is the seduction, where Selene comes to Endymion as he sleeps. But don't worry, you have your eyes closed, since you're supposed to be asleep." He looked down at his brushes with a grin, as Jesse stood quickly from the stool where he had been perched.

"I really can't do this..." he said, but he was still looking at her, his eyes fixed on her face. He always made a point of looking at her eye-to-eye when they were at work, and she wondered why. Perhaps he didn't trust his gaze to venture anywhere else, but how could he possibly avoid it now?

Her nipples stood erect from the touch of the cool wind blowing through the windows, as well as from the attention of her companions. The upsweep of her hair left her neck and shoulders bare, and the trimmed, dark triangle sheltering her womanhood did more to entice than conceal. She was in her element. Grinning, she tilted her chin at him.

"Go on, get undressed."

He shook his head. "This is a bad idea." But he took off his shirt, and his sandals, and his jeans, and finally his briefs.

"Sorry," he said, red-faced.

"It happens," she replied with a dismissing wave. "Don't worry, I won't touch."

"You'd better not," he said with a smile. "Lisa would kill me."

Ah yes: Lisa, the girlfriend; the unimaginative, painted arm-trophy. Another necessary part of the corporate executive uniform.

She laughed. "And that would be bad. Are you ready?"

"As I'll ever be."

She knelt on the metal and glass table that on Will's canvas would become her cloud-tipped mountaintop. The edge of the table felt cold under her bare torso as she stretched out and peered down to where Jesse reclined beneath.

"Hello down there in the mortal world!" she cooed.

He smiled up at her, one arm curved in position beneath his head. With his other hand he reached up around the table's edge and gave her fingertips a friendly tug. "Hello, goddess," he called back. "How are you?"

"Hmm. Olympus is boring and uncomfortable."

He laughed, and shook his head. The pretense of reserve had been abandoned a few weeks ago, as the long afternoons in the lazy intimacy of the studio progressed—a chaste, prolonged foreplay that soothed her secret craving while fueling it even more. She could flirt with him, let her gaze drink in the sight of his nakedness, and imagine what would happen if this table were no longer between them, if his hand strayed to his cock, soft and still deliciously full, waiting to be awakened and to fill her....

"Where is Will, anyway? Still on the phone?"

She blinked. "Yes, I think so." Lifting herself on her elbows, she directed her eyes through the studio doorway. "I can't see him. Oh, wait, here he comes."

Will stuck his head through the studio door and gave them an apologetic look.

"That was my mother. I have to pick my sister up at the airport. John was supposed to do it and he bailed. Figures." He shrugged.

"That's fine, go ahead...."

"Yeah, that's no problem."

"I'm really sorry about this. But hey, you two can have the studio to yourselves now." He grinned. "Just clean up afterward, and lock the door when you leave, OK?"

"Yeah. Right."

"Just for that, we'll be sure not to clean up," added Jesse as Will's head retreated. They heard him laugh as he walked down the hallway, and then the jingle of keys and wallet before the front door slammed shut.

Neither of them moved. They listened to the muffled roar of the car engine, the sound of Will driving off. Her heart beat so hard she was sure he could hear it. No excuse remained for them to be here like this, so dangerously close, without even the modesty of clothing to serve as deterrent.

He was staring up at her as she sat, uncertain, on her pedestal and tried to sort through her thoughts. Wasn't this what she had wanted all along? A perfect opportunity? And it didn't get much more perfect than this. So why was she hesitating again? Not because of their positions; certainly not because of any practical consideration. Because she had wanted this for so long, and because the conquest had not been an easy one. She wasn't sure, this time, that desire alone would be enough. But neither did she want to lose.

"So, are you going to leave now?" she asked softly.

In answer, he slid out from beneath the table and got to his feet. He stood beside the table, looking down at her.

"That all depends on you, goddess."

She had imagined this a thousand times, but the reality of it still overwhelmed her, put her in awe of his body and her own lust. She reached out and closed her hand around his width, her fingertips just barely touching her thumbtip, and she stroked him to fullness. Sticky droplets ran down her fingers, and she felt an answering wet, heavy heat between her legs.

She stood and circled one arm up behind his head, her other hand still moving along his cock. There wasn't much hair to grab, as he kept it short and spiky, and she liked it that way. The less time a man had to spend combing his hair in the morning, the more time he had for getting the job done the night before. But she managed to gain enough of a grip, and tilted his head down.

She would wager he hadn't been kissed like that in a long time, perhaps never. The act was an art, one that few people bothered to take the time to master. But she had. This time she chose to be slow and deliberate, and after a moment of hesitation he kissed her back in kind, running his hands along her waist and over her hips, and then back up to cup her breasts.

He pinched her nipples hard, to the point of pain, of unbearable, unsatisfied hunger. She gasped and broke the kiss with an "Oh!" of pleasure, and he lowered her to the table, pulling her hands away from his groin and moving them up above her head.

His mouth closed around one nipple and then the other, leaving a trail of tiny bites across the curves of her breasts. She had said once, amid the blushing babble of some long-ago, inappropriate water-cooler conversation between them, that she liked biting. All this time, and yet he had remembered; he had been paying attention. She laughed in triumph and pushed down on his shoulders.

He understood and obeyed, lifting her legs and moving to capture her aroused clit between his lips. His tongue moved like witchfire over her sex, teasing the entrance to her slit, slick with her desire, and then moving back up to her clit, and then down…and over and over. His mouth coaxed sweet, pulsing pleasure from her, more than she could have imagined that she would feel lying on the hard, unforgiving studio table. And still she was greedy. She wanted more.

"Fuck me," she murmured.

He lifted his head, and fixed that blue gaze on her. "What? I didn't quite hear that."

"You heard perfectly damn well. I told you to fuck me!"

He smiled, and continued to rub one finger between her nether lips as he bent down to bite each nipple in turn, till she moaned and arched shamelessly against his hand.

"Please, Jesse." Her voice was enticing, pleading, and she was running her nails over his back, and shoulders, and down his chest. "Now."

"God, Arianne, you're too damned hot. It isn't fair."

He grabbed her ass and pulled her toward him. His cock pressed into her, overcoming her body's resistance, and she felt herself opening up, stretching to take him in; painful at first, and then growing softer, moister. She flowed over, and inside, and all around him. His hands were around her waist and he rocked her back and forth with his need.

She closed her eyes, and her body abandoned its form, became nothing but feeling and heat. She was the moon, a center of glowing white light; a wild, rising, rushing elation; and with each thrust of his cock she split into prisms of light. No wonder the ancients thought sex an act of magic, of power. Light splintered all around her in a thousand colored shards.

"Oh, Jesse!"

He leaned his forehead, cool and damp, on hers, breathing in her breath, and lying still, now that the ritual was ended. Purple shadows filled the studio. The sun had been swallowed up by the horizon while they spent their desire.

Now, she thought, would come the awkward separation, the fumbling in the half-dark for artificial light and clothing, while he would look at her with guilt and worry, trying not to meet her gaze.

But instead he only shifted his weight, rolling to lie on his side, his warmth slipping naturally and easily from her body. She sat up and hairpins clattered to the table. He reached back and brushed his fingers through the long tangle of her hair, discarding stray pins that marred the soft waves.

"She was famous for her lovers," he said after a long moment, looking up at her. Even in the poor light she saw his mouth curve into a sensual smile.

"Selene? Yes, she was. But she favored Endymion best of all."

"Mm-hmm. And she kept him around forever, didn't she?"

He tugged gently at her hair and she lay back, marveling at the beauty of his silhouette.

"But he had to choose eternal slumber."

"Can't say that I blame him. I think I would have done the same," he replied. His hand parted her legs and he stroked her still-tingling nexus, sticky now from lovemaking. She was glad she had been wrong this once. He understood that the world of mortals could be left behind, that such lovers as they were created their own immortality. He accepted....

The moon was rising in the sky beyond the windows, climbing to the peak from which it would rush, falling, back to earth again. She was rising.

"Will's probably going to come back soon," he said, pausing, his eyebrows raised in question.

"I know," she said with a wicked grin, and wrapped her arms around his neck again.

CALLIE'S KIDNAPPING

Alyssa Brooks

Callie walked along the side street, her heels clicking with every step. Pausing for just a moment, she straightened her little black dress. God, the thing was so clingy. With her curves, she fell out everywhere. She'd never worn anything like this before. Hell, she'd never *done* anything like this before.

Once again she wondered at herself. Why had she said yes so quickly to her husband this time? Usually she snubbed his wild ideas. Perhaps she was just so tired of being the uptight lawyer. Perhaps she needed a little fun in her life, a little excitement, a little pleasure. A change.

She couldn't deny the anticipation bubbling in her. The thrill of walking down the street, dressed like this, was both scary and exhilarating. The fact that something could go wrong did not escape her. What if someone got the wrong idea about her? What if she ran into a dangerous type?

Sure, it was a decent little city. Still, crime lurked everywhere.

Turing down an alleyway, she blew out a deep breath. Thank goodness that part was over. She'd been so afraid someone would notice her. Recognize her even under her makeup.

Tires came screeching behind her. Whirling around, she saw a black van veering recklessly into the alley. She jumped to the side, out of their way. That was close.

But when they hit their brakes with an awful squeal, she knew they were after her. Her stomach clenched with absolute fear. Panic took over her.

Oh god, oh god, oh god.

She started to run and stumbled over her heels. Kicking them aside, she ran as fast as she could. The rough pavement pained her feet as they slammed into it with every stride. Panting for breath, she fought her mind as it screamed to look back and see who ran after her. Oh god, she had to run faster.

Suddenly a strong arm was wrapping around her waist and yanking her backward. A hand smothered her mouth as she screamed. She was dragged backward, kicking and fighting.

The man pushed her into the van, and she got her first glance at him as he jumped in with her and slammed the door shut. The van took off again; there must be a second captor. The man who held her was tall and well built, with a certain stockiness. His eyes were dark but sharp, like eagle eyes. His lips were wide, plump. Other then that, she was clueless. He wore all black, and even his face was covered by a mask.

"Lie down, now." His voice was gruff and commanding.

She shook as she obeyed him. He climbed over her, grabbed her arms, and stretched them over her head. Then he began to bind them with a black silk cloth. When her hands were tied, he blindfolded her with the same soft material.

The silk could only mean one thing.

Her insides trembled, and the urge to fight invaded her. She bucked under him, but his weight kept her pinned. When she realized how very trapped she was, it scared her even more, and she struggled with everything she had.

"Oh, you're a wild one, all right," the man said with a chuckle.

The van came to a sudden stop and the door opened. She heard another man climb in, but he said not a word. The click of the door locks snapped in the air.

"Roll over, get on your knees."

It occurred to her that she could continue to fight, but it would only anger them. Perhaps if she obeyed them, this would be quick and painless. Trepidation trembled in her as she obeyed the command.

Strong hands immediately pushed up her dress. Underneath she wore no underwear. Fingers pressed into her, and spread her apart. Gasping, she jerked forward. A sharp slap bit into her ass.

Then she felt a cock prodding at her mouth. The same man spoke to her. "You'd better be good and please us. You don't want to test our patience."

She knew she had no choice. Opening her mouth to him, she swallowed his cock as the other man played with her pussy. The cock slid in and out of her throat as the other's fingers pushed inside her.

The man's thumb kneaded her clit and, despite herself, arousal pooled in her. She began to get wet under his exploration faster then she ever had before. Then his tongue began to explore her lips. Sensation poured through her, and her only venue to express it was through the cock in her mouth. She began to lick and swirl her tongue around it, swallowing deeply.

Moans escaped her. Strong need built in her, and the situation only fueled her desire. The man behind her withdrew his mouth, grabbed her ass, and kneaded it in his hands. With one strong thrust, his cock invaded her body. She cried out and went into an immediate orgasm.

Her body convulsed with pleasure.

The orgasm faded, but her ecstasy did not. She was so wet, so wanton. She bucked against him. Her ass slapped against his hips. The other cock rammed in and out of her greedy mouth.

She joined both men in another peak. Her mouth filled with seed at the same moment the man behind her squirted his hot come all over her ass. Exhausted, she collapsed. A sharp slap bit into her butt.

"You aren't done yet," said the first man. Pulling his cock from her mouth, he shuffled in back of her. "Back on your knees. *Now.*"

The man from the back now moved to her front, grasped her by her hair, and pulled her head up. His cock, slippery with her own juices, pushed into her mouth.

Another smack fired on her ass. She cried out, and moved back onto her knees. There was no choice but to obey. The concept filled her with a second wind, and new want.

Thrusting her ass in the air, she welcomed his cock as she sucked on the other. He drove into her with one hard plunge.

She rammed against him, and almost immediately came. Both men jerked inside her and filled her with their release.

Once again, her body collapsed. The man in front of her pulled up his zipper, and she listened to him open the van door, which he then shut behind him.

He was gone. She'd never heard his voice. She'd never seen his face. And she never would. That had been part of the deal.

She rolled onto her back. The other man untied her wrists and removed her blindfold. With a smile, she gazed up at her husband.

"Thank you, darling," he said, reaching out to caress her leg. "That was great."

"I have to admit, it was. I was so nervous."

"Do you think you could do it again?"

"Surprise me," she said with a light laugh. It was a new part of her—this sexual, uninhibited woman he was bringing out in her. It would take some getting used to, but she liked this part of herself.

Perhaps one day she would even surprise *him*.

THE GUY YOUR MOTHER WARNED YOU ABOUT

Chris Costello

I drew some dirty looks as I walked into the club, which gave me a thrill. I could practically feel my cock throbbing in my pants as I leered at all the beautiful girls—and I felt I should be embarrassed for having a hard-on. How long would it take them to make me, I wondered? Longer than I thought, as it turned out, because nobody came over and sat next to me, and Karita, the cocktail waitress, cast nary a glance in my direction.

Fuck, I thought. *I did it.*

Looked like nobody I knew well had decided to show up that night; that was probably part of the reason nobody spotted me. But I guess I still must have looked pretty convincing to get that kind of attitude from the waitress.

Now, the acid test, after ten minutes of waiting and two cigarettes—Marlboros, of course: "Hey, could I get a Hefeweisen over here?" I shouted at the top of my lungs, over the L7 blaring from the speakers. To me, my voice sounded squeaky, girly, too feminine—but the nasty look I got from Karita told me I was doing fine.

Karita was a twenty-something punkette like me, only way more femme than I could ever hope to be (or want to). She was wearing a tight pair of leather pants that laced up the sides and a tight, low-cut, bright red tank top that said, I'M THE GUY YOUR MOTHER WARNED YOU ABOUT. It was cut off just below her breasts. She looked even better than usual, and my practiced male swagger made me want to leer at those full breasts, pretty face, and bee-stung lips in a weirdly entitled fashion. I felt I had every right to walk up to this distant acquaintance and bury my face between her breasts, just because I wanted to—which was something I had never felt in my life.

Feeling like that was making me incredibly wet.

It was an empty night at the CoCo Club—maybe twenty, twenty-five women lounging about in various stages of festivity, a few of them dressed up, but most in their casual Sunday clothes: jeans, T-shirts, sharkskin jackets, leather, the uniform of mostly-under-thirty San Francisco dykes on the make. Sexy, tough, rugged. Hip.

There in the corner, though, sat the girl of my dreams. She was pale and gorgeous, femme and curvy and more than a little slutty-looking, an impression she obviously cultivated. She always dressed up—I'd never seen her without heels, makeup, and her hair done up with that messy just-fucked look she liked to work. Tonight the girl was wearing a tight little red dress that would have been a slip on a more proper girl, and just barely that. I could see her breasts, braless, and her panty lines through the tight red slip, which for some reason my inner lech found incredibly sexy. She was also wearing a red feather boa casually draped around her shoulders, a trademark I'd seen on her more than a few times. Her stockings were black fishnet, the lace tops and garters visible just under the lace hem of the slip, and she had what must have been four-inch heels.

Karita and a couple of other people had told me her name was Danielle, but we'd never been formally introduced. Still, we'd flirted more than a few times, and how I'd never managed to even get an introduction was beyond me, especially now that I was pumped up on imaginary male hormones. I resolved to walk up to her and introduce myself, then suddenly felt the butterflies in my stomach that had taken me over the last three times I'd tried. It's not as if Danielle hadn't given me more than a few smoldering looks, but I was supposed to be the butch here, wasn't I?

Not that I was a *real* butch, most of the time—oh, I tried for that hard-edged swagger and a sneering chuckle, but a perky, boyish bounce and a red-faced and vaguely unfeminine giggle were the best I'd been able to manage. Tonight was different, though—I wasn't just butch, I was a sexist pig and itinerant male oppressor, so Danielle could bloody well blow me. I'd barely had that thought when I saw her looking at me with a smirk on her face—had she made me? Or was she just so impressed by my cojones in walking in here that she figured I was cool, even if I *was* a party-crashing straight dude? God, she was fucking gorgeous—big brown eyes and long black hair contrasted hard against her pale skin, lips painted the color of blood. I wanted to taste those lips so bad it hurt.

Karita took her time with my beer, finally sauntering over well after I'd cracked the *Sports Illustrated* swimsuit issue I'd brought along—the finishing touch, in case I failed to piss anyone off. When Karita came over, she told me, much colder than the beer, "Three-fifty."

I handed her a five. "Here you go, dollface," I said in my gruff voice, and patted her ass. "You can keep the change."

That's when she made me—lucky thing, too, because her fist

was already balled up. Dykes like Karita don't slap.

She bent forward and peered into my face.

"Chris?" she asked tentatively.

"The name's Chad," I told her. "That's a great pair of pants you're wearing, honey. Nice top, too. And I like what's in it. You know, I really *am* the guy your mother warned you about. What time do you get off?"

"Oh, I'm getting off right now," she said through a wicked smile. "Don't worry, I won't blow your cover, but you're about to get lynched on the dance floor if nobody but me takes a closer look."

I crushed out my cigarette. "Thanks, Sweet-cheeks," I said, hoping she didn't see me go pale. "You need a big comfortable lap to sit on later, you know where to find me."

"Oh, I'll find you," she replied. "But I have the feeling Danny's going to find you first."

A chill went down my spine. Some leather fag bouncer they'd hired, maybe?

"Danny?"

"Danielle," said Karita. "Don't tell me you haven't seen the way she's looking at you, Chad."

Danielle was staring, her chin propped on her fist, her eyes roving over me from across the bar.

I reddened.

Karita disappeared and I drank half my Hefeweisen in one gulp. I tried to light another Marlboro and found my hands were shaking. I told myself this was too crazy, I couldn't just walk over there and turn on the charm like some tough-guy. I couldn't even change the fucking oil on my Kia Sephia, for God's sake. All right, I would have two more beers and then I'd go up and introduce myself to Danielle as Chris, she'd recognize me, I'd take off the mustache, I'd slip off the sharkskin suit and the suspenders, unknot the tie, and take off the dress shirt so she could see my slight breasts in the white undershirt I wore, know it was really me. Then we'd have a laugh over it and maybe I could ask for her phone number, take her to the film festival the week after next. That was always good for a first date. No way was I going to play this charade of drag-king swagger with a girl I actually liked—that would be stupid; she'd never go for it. That sort of thing would seem silly to an accomplished glam queen like Danielle.

"Excuse me, sir?"

I looked up from my beer and my ears popped; all of a sudden I felt dizzy and nauseous.

"Y–yes?"

"I don't believe we've been introduced," said Danielle, standing closer to me than I expected—so close I could smell her perfume even over the cigarette smoke and beer and sweat of the bar. What was it? Something I recognized, something my older sister Candace had worn to her junior prom.

"I'm Danielle." She put out her hand, palm down.

I remembered my manners and stood. "I'm Chad," I said, grasping her hand, touching my lips to it, and lingering a bit too long. "Chad…Costello." I found myself taking a deep breath, sniffing up her arm like some character from a Bugs Bunny cartoon. I turned her hand over and smelled her wrist, finally placing the scent.

"Chanel No. 5," I said. Now *that's* femme. "A beautiful scent for a beautiful woman." My heart was pounding and I felt like I was about to faint—or throw up on her. That wouldn't have been very butch at all.

"Oh, Mr. Costello," said Danielle, making a show of hiding her face and even blushing a little bit—how the hell did she manage that?—even while her eyes showed a wicked sparkle and she licked her lips sexily. "You're flattering me. I always get so embarrassed when men flatter me!"

"I'm sure it happens a lot," I said. "And please call me Chad."

"Oh, I couldn't," she said. "We've just met. I don't want to seem, you know, *that* way."

"Oh, there's nothing wrong with being that way," I said. "And besides, we're going to get a lot more familiar, you know." Fuck, had I actually said that? Impossible. Feeling drunk with power and fear, I said, "Please sit down."

She moved to sit in the chair across from me and I gently grasped her arm. "Not there," I said, hardly believing I was doing this. I patted my lap. "It's much more comfortable over here."

"Oh, I couldn't." She managed to suppress the ironic smile that played at the edge of her mouth. I could see her nipples through the thin silk of her slip—harder than before? Was this turning her on? I knew I was so wet I could have slid right out of my chair.

"Please," I said, and Danielle didn't have to be asked a third time. She settled into my lap and draped her arms around my shoulders, her breasts just inches from my face and straining to get through that lacy slip. She playfully twined her feather boa around my neck and tickled my nose with the other end. I breathed deeply of her scent and felt my cunt respond, my nipples pressing against the Ace bandage I'd used to bind my breasts. I knew from the way Danielle was sitting that she could feel the bulge of the precariously arranged dildo strapped to my body and stuffed into my jockstrap—and in case I had any doubts, she began to squirm against it, rubbing her ass against my cock as if casually, though there was nothing casual about it.

I looked up into Danielle's delectable face, hoping I didn't look too much like a schoolgirl in love. To cover my consternation, I let one hand rest unceremoniously on the place where her ass rested on my knee, and brought my other hand up to her thigh, placing it at the spot where her garters met her lace-top fishnets, right at the lace hem of her slip, so much so that my thumb even went underneath the garment. I smiled up at her mischievously, like an adolescent boy doing something bad, which is how I felt—the part of me that wasn't terrified she'd slug me and my chances would be ruined.

But she didn't slug me, didn't pull away. Instead, she snuggled closer, letting her breasts hover ever nearer my face while she ran her fingers through my hair. She cocked her head and breathed seductively into my ear.

"Waitress," I shouted. "Get this lady a drink!" Then, softer, "What're you drinking, Danielle?"

"Cosmopolitan."

"One cosmo!" I called out to Karita. Then to Danielle I said, "You must watch that HBO show with all those horny women."

"In bed with my clothes off," said Danielle with a smile. "Every fucking week."

Karita brought the cosmopolitan and another beer, and I held up a ten.

"On the house," said Karita. "Dykes with balls get special consideration."

"Then go buy yourself something lacy, dollface," I said, holding out the ten.

Karita smiled. "Oh, you mean it, Mr. Costello?" She set down the tray of drinks on an adjacent table and put both hands on her tits, pushing them together and bending forward until she could pluck the bill away with her cleavage. She did exactly that, and I didn't even move the $10 to make it any easier for her. A couple of women across the bar hooted and applauded as Karita came away with the ten-spot stuck between her breasts at the slight *V* of her tank top. I guess by then they'd figured out I wasn't a tourist. Karita bent forward and gave me a kiss on the lips.

"Whore," Danielle said to her, putting one hand on my cheek. "Get your own man." She kissed me, too, her full lips meeting mine and her slender tongue teasing its way into my mouth as Karita made a snide comment—"That's what I was doing, slut"—and danced away.

Danielle's lips parted with mine and she smiled.

"You don't know what a thrill it is to get a man in here," she cooed. "I mean a *real* man." She squirmed some more against my cock.

"I guess you don't get many guys in here," I said gruffly. "I mean, in *this* kind of a club."

She giggled, kissed my ear. "Well, you know.... The management does sort of discourage it. We never know when a virile guy like yourself might walk in and steal all the femmes away."

"Is that right?"

"Oh, yes. You know how we are. We'll come here, all right, but we're just waiting for the right man to come in, drag us home by the hair, and throw us on the bed. That's what we all want, isn't it? Even if we don't know it."

"Oh. Is that what *you* want?"

She looked into my eyes, her big brown ones seducing me in a way I'd never been seduced before. I could smell the liquor on her breath—

I tried to suppress my guffaw, which didn't work—instead, it turned into a giggle, as if I were a six-year-old playing dress-up with her best friend. I couldn't stop giggling. I started coughing to hide the sound, and to cover my nervousness I slipped my hand even further up Danielle's dress. Now I could feel the soft skin of her thigh, and I found myself noticing that with my other hand I couldn't feel those panty lines that had so turned me on when they showed through her slip. I ran my fingertips over the heart-shape of her ass and wondered aloud at their absence.

"I took them off," she whispered into my ear. "I thought you'd like that. I know how a tough guy like you doesn't like to waste time undressing a woman."

Now my head was spinning for real, and I thought I actually might pass out. I tried hard not to blush, but as we sat there and drank our drinks, Danielle's flirting increased a notch as we traded double entendres and brushed our bodies against each other. I got wetter with every sultry caress she gave the back of my neck, with every time she ran her fingers through my hair, with every kiss she planted on my lips. I had come in here planning to bewitch with my arrogance and braggadocio, but now this femme was seducing me with all the subtlety of Marilyn Monroe on ecstasy. I can't say I minded.

"You ever been with a *real* man?" I asked her in between flirts and kisses, in between letting my hands casually graze her breasts as I held her.

"Oh, I turn them *into* real men," she said, kissing my forehead.

"Think you could pull that trick with me?" I asked.

"Oh, I won't need to," she said. "I could tell that right away."

I still don't remember how we made it from the table at the CoCo Club to the stairway leading up to the street. The four or five drinks probably helped, but I would have taken this girl home even if I'd been drinking ginger ale.

On the sidewalk, I helped Danielle on with her long leather

coat, feeling a sadness as I watched her button that gorgeous body away from me like a present wrapped before Christmas—as if I was never going to get a chance to unwrap it.

"I don't live far," she said in a tiny voice.

"Good," I told her. "My wife is waiting for me at home."

She giggled and led me toward the nearby alley. The truth was that my three roommates were probably waiting up for me, and would razz me till the end of time if I came home with a sweet thing like Danielle on my arm.

The second we got in the alley, though, I found myself seized with a sudden urgency. I glanced around to make sure no one was watching—it was midnight on a Sunday night, and the streets were largely empty—then grabbed Danielle and pushed her up against the brick wall behind the dumpster, kissing her and thrusting my hand roughly under her dress. She was wearing hardly anything underneath.

"Mr. Costello, please...," she sighed, squirming against me as I touched her smooth pussy. "Someone might see."

"That's the idea," I growled, slipping one finger inside her as I kissed her hard, as she moaned and wriggled against the brick wall and rubbed her tits against my chest. I couldn't believe how wet she was—almost as wet as I was.

The alley was open to the street but darker and fairly hard to see from it. I knew more than a few girls who did things in this alley, but I'd never done it myself. I guess I never got drunk enough, or horny enough. No, wait, I know I was horny enough—I just wasn't a heavy drinker. But any guy named Chad Costello wouldn't hesitate to take his woman in an alley, right? Well, at least, that was my fantasy.

I slipped my hand out of Danielle's crotch, brought it to my mouth, and licked it. Then she licked it, too, and we kissed hungrily around my finger and the sharp taste of her pussy. I pushed my sharkskin-clad leg up between Danielle's legs and shoved it hard into her crotch. She clamped her thighs around my knee and whimpered as I fucked her with my leg. The world smelled like piss and garbage, but all I could smell was Chanel No. 5. I dropped to my knees and slipped both my hands up under Danielle's dress, pulling it almost to her waist. There really wasn't much under there—it looked like she meticulously shaved her pussy. But there was everything I needed.

I pushed Danielle against the side of the dumpster, easing her ass up onto the little shelf so she could spread her legs wider, and buried my face between her spread thighs. I slid my tongue between her swollen lips and tasted the sharp tang of her juice, which was dribbling out as fast as I could lap it up. I teased my way up to her clit and suckled it gently into my mouth, flicking my tongue tip violently up and down against it in a quickening rhythm.

"Oh god," she moaned, and gripped my hair to pull my face harder into her.

"More," she whimpered. "Harder. Do it harder."

I sucked as hard as I could and lapped my tongue rhythmically up on her clit, working the tip under the hood so I could get to her most sensitive spot. Every time I did, I was rewarded with a shuddering groan of ecstasy, and we no longer cared who saw or heard. I licked faster and Danielle threw her head back, hitting it hard on the corner of the dumpster so the whole thing rang like a Chinese gong.

"You all right?" I asked suddenly, looking up.

"Don't stop!" she gasped as she grabbed the edge of the dumpster and lifted both her legs all the way into the air. "Don't! I'm going to come!"

So I merged my mouth once more with her pussy and brought her over the edge, feeling her thighs closing on my head like a nutcracker and her body twisting atop me as she spasmed. Her feather boa dislodged itself somehow and dropped down around my shoulders, its ends coiling on the ground. Danielle kept moaning "Fuck me, fuck me, fuck me" as she came, so when I felt the rhythmic convulsions of her body slowing and stopping, I put one hand on her belly to keep her from falling off the container and pulled myself up with the other. I wedged her against the dumpster with my body and reached down to unzip my pants.

She stared into my eyes, her face and breasts flushed with the aftermath of her orgasm. She had the hungry look of a woman who wants to be fucked so bad she'll die if she doesn't get it in the next ten seconds. I must have taken fifteen or twenty fumbling with my belt and slacks and jockstrap, because she closed her eyes and looked away, sounding like she was sobbing hysterically as she gasped, "Fuck me, fuck me, fuck me!"

Then I had my dick in my hand, and I leaned back to let a long stream of spit dribble onto the head.

"Oh god," she moaned. "Yeah. Fuck me."

I rubbed the spittle-slick head against Danielle's clit a few times, feeling her body explode every time I did. Was she too sensitive for that right after coming so hard? I didn't even care. I was going to fuck her the way I wanted to fuck her, and something told me that was exactly what she wanted, too. I teased her mercilessly, making her beg me a dozen times and more.

"Put it in," she whimpered over and over again. "God, please, put it in me. I need your cock."

Then I nuzzled it against the entrance to her cunt and pushed it in, feeling her postclimax tightness clamp hard against my entry. I got it into her and started fucking her, slow at first, then faster as she begged me.

"Harder," she whispered into my ear. "Fuck me harder, Mr.

Costello. Fuck me like I don't matter. Make yourself come inside me."

So I did, pounding into her as hard as I could, until I heard her moaning again and I knew from the shuddering of her body that she was coming a second time. So I threw back my head and made the gruffest, most masculine grunt I could manage, and grunted: "I'm gonna come, baby, I'm gonna come in your pussy!" Then I realized I had no fucking idea what a guy felt like when he came, or what his body moved like—not the faintest clue what I should do when I shot my load in Danielle's pussy. But as if from Heaven, my roommate Tony's fag porn came to me in a rush—barely academic interest when I watched it, mind you, but now I could remember the frenzied motions of the leatherboys as they came on each other. I tried to approximate that, shuddering in just that way and thundering, "Oh, yeah!" as I came.

When we ground to a halt, Danielle slumped against me, kissing my neck. "I still don't live far," she told me.

So I pulled down her dress and buttoned up my sharkskin slacks, and buckled my belt and led her by the hand away from the stinking dumpster I'd just fucked her against. I stopped when I saw Karita leaning up against the doorway to the club, smoking a cigarette.

"I'm sorry," she said, breathing smoke. "You were making so much noise I just couldn't resist. I hope you don't mind?"

I looked at Danielle, who shrugged and smiled. I shrugged, too. Danielle leaned over, gave Karita a quick kiss on the lips and said, "But you may *not* come home with us—at least not tonight."

Karita laughed nervously, and so did I—a very unmasculine sound. Danielle and I left Karita standing there smoking in the alley, and walked the four blocks to Danielle's apartment.

COPS AND ROBBERS

KC

I still can't take my eyes off you. The party is packed with people wearing the most outrageous costumes I've ever seen—drag queens dolled up with yard-high bouffants, Anita Bryant spanking RuPaul with a big wooden cutting board. There are three Martha Stewarts and more fetching hookers, schoolgirls, and coquettes than you could shake a stick at, about evenly divided between women and men in their twenties, thirties, and forties.

But you're the one I can't take my eyes off, because you look like nothing I've ever expected.

You were so secretive about your costume, stashing it at work, blowing off my questions with vague smiles, giving me just the most tantalizing of hints. But I had no idea. I really had no idea. When you walked out of the bathroom wearing that outfit, I just about flipped. Your knee-high motorcycle boots were polished till they gleamed, and their heels added a good two inches to your already impressive height. Your tan pants fit tight and flawlessly, the dark stripe outlining your long, muscled legs. You had the helmet, too, complete with microphone. Your belt had everything it was supposed to have: ammo cases packed with condoms, a fake gun. And handcuffs.

I could see myself in your mirrored aviator sunglasses. I could see my eyes wide, my face blushing red. And I hadn't even put my costume on yet.

I'll never know, I guess, if you dropped some hint that made me think in terms I wouldn't have otherwise thought. I'll never know if I guessed, subconsciously, that you were going to be the vibrant cream of the law-enforcement crop for the costume party, and so, if I wanted to get my fondest wish I'd better be something naughty too.

You remember those fast-food commercials from the '70s, don't you? The ones with the character who was always trying to steal hamburgers? I'm a little embarrassed that my costume was so silly, but it got lots of compliments from the big-haired drag queens, so I guess it must have worked. Besides, I'd gone out of my way to make it sexy, and I hoped it would have the desired effect on you in particular.

The cape and the hat were easy to come by. I went without the fake mustache because however cheesy I was, I wanted to be a sexy '70s icon, after all. The striped outfit was a little more difficult. I found one at a costume shop, but it fit me like a canvas sack, so I sewed my own, skintight and low-cut, clinging to every curve of my body. On any other night, it would have been almost obscene.

I guess it's just a sort of poetic justice that I'm a vegetarian.

As I sit there in the big armchair, watching the party go by, I'm quite aware that I should have used thicker material for the top.

My nipples are hard from watching you. They show plainly through the striped top, which has grown damp with my sweat in the close quarters of the costume party. The room is reasonably dark, but ultraviolet lights over by the punch bowl are igniting the fires in my white stripes, making my nipples stand out more clearly, making me feel more exposed. Some guy is trying to talk to me, leaning close, glancing from my face to my tits and back again. He's some dot-com reject with a hard-on for hamburgers, I guess.

I make polite conversation, searching for you in the crowd as you sway in and out of my vision, fending off (I hope) all the svelte hookers and buxom schoolgirls trying to tempt you away from me. I catch a glimpse of you and my breath halts; I can see the rapt face of a pigtailed slut reflected in your sunglasses. I feel my pulse quickening as I watch you flirt with her. I wonder if you're thinking about taking her home with us. The guy leaning close to me asks me if I'd like to go somewhere. I tell him I'm here with someone and he falls all over himself apologizing, like I care. I smile at him, tell him I'm going to go find my friends, and say it was nice to meet him.

Threading through the crowd, I find myself lost; I can't find you. I've been planning it since I first saw you in your outfit, but I thought I'd be able to wait until we got home. Now I know I can't wait; I've got to have you *now*.

I've been planning it, running over and over the fantasy in my mind: going up to you, putting my lips to your ear and saying, "I want to turn myself in, Officer."

But now I can't find you. The press of bodies crushes me as an ancient '70s disco anthem comes on, remixed for a circuit party from hell. A drag queen grabs me and tries to get me to dance. I beg off, blushing, pushing away. "Got to go steal some hamburgers," I say weakly. I feel a hand on my ass and I start to turn, not knowing if I'm going to reproach some playful queen or slap some sleazy straight boy.

Instead, I find that I can't turn, because you've got me pinned, holding my slim wrists easily in one of your big hands. I'm immobile, pulled hard up against your body, smelling the leather of your jacket as it overpowers the scent of bodies, pot, and liquor.

I feel your breath hot against my neck as you growl into my ear:

"I suggest you turn yourself in, Ma'am."

I melt, just like that. I'm yours; you could do anything you wanted to me. But when I feel the handcuffs going around my wrists, hear you ratcheting them tight between beats of house music, that's when I really feel it start: the heat between my legs, the almost painful throb, the flood of moisture that soaks the too-thin material of my tights. God, everyone will know. Everyone will know I'm wet. It'll soak right through my tights and everyone will know how wet you make me, how bad I want you to handcuff me and fuck me so hard I scream, so hard I cry. Everyone will know.

And if anyone doesn't notice you French-walking me down the hallway, it's not because of any discretion on your part—it's because they're too lost in their own drunken gropes and coke-addled dancing to notice a straight couple locked in a heated rendition of the quintessential bondage scenario: cops and robbers.

By the time you usher me into the bedroom, I'm so wet you can probably smell me. You toss me onto the huge pile of jackets, leather, and faux fur mingling against me as I wriggle in my handcuffs. Every time I feel the sharp pull of the metal against my wrists, a new wave of pleasure goes through me. Helpless, I'm helpless. I hear you lock the deadbolt.

You lean on me, hard, your hand thrust between my tightly closed legs. But you're too strong, and your hand forces its way in there. When you run your fingers over my pussy, I know that I was right: I have soaked through my tights. I knew I should have worn underwear, panty lines or no. The tights are so wet anyone could have seen them if they'd cared to look. And maybe they did.

Your mirrored eyes flash the light of the lava lamp, and you smile. It's that smile that always melts me, but I'm already melted, reduced to a quivering pool of need here on the leather-strewn bed.

"Do you know what the punishment is for attempted theft of a hot beef injection, Ma'am?"

I want to giggle, I want to—really. It's funny. But my breath catches in my throat, because now you're pressing on my cunt, working the swollen mounds of my lips, rubbing your finger on my erect clit.

"No, Officer," I manage to croak. "What is the punishment?"

"Whatever I want it to be," you growl, mercilessly toying with me. I am so completely at your mercy that you could have me any way you want, and you know it. I can feel how much you know it by the firm shaft of your cock pressing through your skintight pants as you lean on me. But you're having too much fun torturing me to just take me. You've got much crueler things in mind for me.

My tights are around my ankles in an instant, and the soft boots I wore are gone in a jumble of soaked, stretchy stripes, leaving me barefoot and naked from the waist down. I try to close my thighs, but your knee is wedged between them and you force my left leg far open, leaning over to get your arm around my right thigh. I'm spread, helpless. I'm open for you, unable to stop you from doing whatever you want with my pussy.

I struggle against the handcuffs, moaning softly as I await my punishment. Then I feel it.

The first open-handed blow is soft; I could have handled something much harder, and you knew it from experience. But this time it takes my breath away, because your big, broad hand doesn't connect with the sweet spot of my ass—it lands squarely on my pussy. If you'd hit me any harder, I think I would have come right then.

I writhe in your grasp, pushing back against your hand, lifting my ass in the air. My breasts, braless and covered only by the thin, low-cut top, rub against the faux fur and leather, my nipples so hard that they send shivers through my body as they catch on buttons and zippers. You no longer need to wrestle my thighs apart; with that one blow on my cunt, you rendered me utterly unable to resist you. But you still hold me tight, reminding me that you're in control, that there's nothing I can do to stop you. And that excites me still more, making my cunt purr and pulse with desire.

You spank my pussy again, this time a little harder. With your middle finger extended slightly like that, you're stimulating my tormented clit with every blow. I hear myself whimpering like an animal, wriggling and squirming underneath you. You spank me again. I pull against the handcuffs, their pressure heightening my arousal. Again. I can feel the pleasure building inside me, coming closer and closer as I get ready to let go.

You spank me again, harder still, mounting my pleasure toward orgasm without caring whether or not I want to come. You've never spanked my pussy together; every other time I lay there spread in your lap and let you take your liberties with my ass, making me squirm and writhe with every blow on my sweet spot, I've never felt this. Never felt this merciless rush toward orgasm, as I feel the sudden blows coming faster and faster on my pussy, making me moan, squirm, and lose control.

I throw my head back, my wrists tight in the handcuffs, and wail helplessly as I come. I can feel your cock grinding hard against my body as you spank me faster and faster, forcing my orgasm into the stratosphere. I'm practically in tears from pleasure by the time you slow and then stop, placing your warm hand on my pussy, feeling me shudder underneath you.

I'm mewling wordlessly, my capacity for communication lost as I feel the echoes of the orgasm go through my body. I'm hardly aware of that big belt being unbuckled, your big cock being slipped out of those skintight tan pants. But when I feel you mounting me, feel the thick head of your cock sliding between my swollen cunt-lips, I know what's coming, and I push back onto you desperately, forcing myself onto your cock.

My ass presses against you as you slide your cock home, pushing it into me until I feel it firmly on my G-spot, bringing a moan and a gasp from me as you start to fuck me hungrily, your hands grasping my bound wrists, your hips pumping wildly. Now that I've come, I'm your prisoner, a captured criminal, and you're taking your pleasure with me, not caring if I want it. Maybe that's why I feel it coming on so quickly—my second orgasm. Maybe that's why I lift myself onto my knees, ass pressed down close to my ankles, giving me leverage to push so hard back onto you, fucking myself onto your cock as you meet each thrust of my body with one of your own.

When we're making love, we rarely come at the same time. Now, though, both of us are so turned on that we couldn't stop our oncoming orgasms if we wanted to. We pound against each other, your cock throbbing deep inside me as I feel the head of it hitting my cervix. Then I'm coming, and begging you for your come, which you give me as your body tenses, then releases with a smooth round of easy thrusts into me, making me come harder as I feel your cock pulsing, filling me.

When you pull out of me, I slump forward on the pile of coats, my mouth open, drooling on a faux-fur Nehru jacket. I look back at you over my shoulder, still wanting you, feeling the ache where your cock has slipped out of me.

You smile, those mirrored eyes reflecting the slackness of my face, all resistance fucked out of me. I'm your prisoner, ready for further punishment.

You smile.

"Now that makes a nice mug shot," you tell me mischievously.

And looking into my own eyes, four of them reflected in your mirrored sunglasses, I have to agree.

MR. RIGHT(S)

Ayre Riley

I broke up in a rush. The finale was one year coming and one minute ending. He said I'd blown it big time. He said that if I'd played my cards right, I would have lived happily ever after, like a fairy tale. He said that he was my prince, my Mr. Right. What had I done to earn his anger? The first two years together, I'd been his humble student, soaking up everything he taught me. The second two, I'd rebelled and attempted to be myself. I didn't agree with him by default. I fought. I clawed. Ultimately, I guess I won: freedom. But not the ending to our fairy tale.

"Go on home," he demanded. "Go back to Mommy and Daddy."

I didn't.

I ended up moving in momentarily with a girlfriend and her two male roommates. And after four stifling years of living with the wrong man, I couldn't wait to be with a right one. Either one her roommates would have been right. They were both goodlooking, both a little older than me, but not too old. Not as old as my ex. They both checked me out when I dropped my one small suitcase on the floor of the guestroom, and I caught interested looks in their eyes.

I felt on fire. I felt as if I would explode if I didn't get next to a man. I didn't want a relationship. I'd had plenty of what that word meant. I wanted good, hot sex, because in four years I hadn't had any.

And in the way only fairy tales usually end, I got precisely what I wanted. My first Mr. Right was tall and slim, an actor with dark eyes and dark curly hair. He had a look that was half-seductive, half-devilish. I could tell he was bad news as far as women were concerned, the type of player who could turn women off men, in general. At any other time, I would have known to avoid him. Instead, I went on my knees in front of him and undid the button fly of his jeans. He said nothing. He didn't look surprised or eager. He looked accepting, which is exactly what I needed. I wanted to be accepted. Accepted for my greedy, sinful desires. I got out his cock, and gazed at his erection for a minute before sliding my lips around the head. He ran his fingers through my long black hair, caressed my slim shoulders through my silky blue-and-white checked pajamas. He moaned softly and whispered sounds of deep encouragement.

When had I last sucked cock?

Didn't remember. That's how long it had been. And not for lack of trying, either. My ex intellectualized sex. He wanted Tantric orgasms. He wanted our souls to be as one. Nice thought, that. But I wanted heat. I wanted quick, ferocious fuck sessions, and I wanted nights of sweaty, unstopping, heartpounding sex. The type that makes you weak for days. The type that makes you forget to eat. That puts dark circles under your eyes. That makes you radiate.

Had I ever sucked cock in a living room, where two other roommates had the potential of walking in at any moment and disturbing us? That was easy to answer: no. I felt like a co-ed again, and really, at only twenty-two, I *could* have been a co-ed still. But what I felt most was free and untamed, and all because I had a stranger's thick, hard cock in my mouth.

Not a *real* stranger. He was Jean's roommate, after all. But who was Jean? Someone I sort of knew from work. She was a half-assed acquaintance rather than a real friend. And who was I to be doing this so boldly on the revolting green shag rug in her living room after she was kind enough to let me move in for a few weeks? Nobody that I recognized. Nobody that I'd been introduced to. But maybe that was the point. I was ready not to be me anymore. That was the fantasy. That was the fairy tale.

My ex had been unduly concerned with appearances. What will it look like if you travel somewhere on your own? How will it look if you quit your job here and search for a different one? How will it look? *How will it look?* For the first time in four years, I didn't care about appearances. I didn't care if someone saw us. If someone walked in. If someone judged me.

Like I didn't care later on in the night when Ian left for a hot date with a actress he'd met at an audition, and Paul took his place on the sofa. And I took my spot automatically on the floor in front of him, as if it was the proper place for me. Good girl, on her knees again, ready to drink from another stranger's cock.

He was wearing dove-gray sweatpants and I pulled them down and freed his dick. He was hard before I had my warm fist wrapped fully around him, hard before I glanced up at his face to make sure that this was okay with him. He had a different expression from his roommate's. Tousle-haired Paul was clearly not someone who expected such treatment, but someone who was extremely glad that he was getting it.

I sucked him happily, taking my time. I slid my tongue from root to head, then back again, swirled my tongue around the shaft, bestowed on him the attention I'd been longing to give someone—anyone—for so long. I teased him and taunted him, using all those long-repressed sexual tricks, stroking his balls gently while I sucked like a powerhouse. I made him cry out when he came, and I swallowed every drop. Then, after giving him the time to regain his composure, I made him come again.

It was as if I was trying to wash away a bad taste—the bad taste of a four-year relationship gone indisputably sour—and the only way I could think to do it was to blow these two amazingly handsome men. Two in one night. One right after the other.

And as I did, I realized that my ex couldn't have been more wrong. Because now I could see what lay in store for me. My happily ever after.

And all my future Mr. Rights.

FORCE OF NATURE

Miranda Austin

They had been anticipating the encounter for weeks, ever since a whispered exchange of fantasies had revealed this startling coincidence of desires. They didn't talk about it much after the first discussion, wanting the actual event to be as spontaneous as possible. But the very thought drove them to distraction, day and night, until they finally arranged for the house to be empty one Saturday. They had planned to wait until dark, but by mid-afternoon they could no longer stand it.

"Why don't you get changed?" he suggested. Her insides squirmed, but she nodded. Hugging him once, she disappeared into their bedroom and shut the door.

She had been trying to decide what to wear for days. Usually she slept in the nude, but they had agreed that a proper "rapist" needs clothing to tear off. Suddenly there was no more time to plan. Her hands rummaged through the dresser drawer, bypassing her favorite silk pajamas, until she found the plain green cotton nightshirt and matching briefs. Yes, perfect.

She sat on the bed, shivering, clutching the nightgown. She could still back out—all she had to do was open the door and tell him she'd changed her mind. They could order in Chinese food, maybe watch a movie, and make gentle love in front of the fireplace. But no, she wasn't going to chicken out. She wanted this too much.

It felt strange and sexy to slide between the sheets, knowing that sometime soon a ruthless assailant would be breaking in to have his wicked way with her. She fidgeted under the blanket, pressing her already-moist thighs together, trying to decide whether she should lie on her front or her back, settling on her stomach so she wouldn't be able to see him when he came in. She hesitated when reaching for the light switch—once the lights were off, he'd know she was ready—and at the last second she slid the lamp as far away from the bed as it would go. They definitely did not need broken glass and ceramic interrupting them.

The closed blinds gave a reasonable illusion of night. Determinedly she ignored the mounting urge to slip her hand down to her pussy. It wouldn't do for him to break in and find her playing with herself! How long would he make her wait? She shut her eyes, calmed her breathing, and, against all odds, actually started drifting off.

After what seemed like a long time, but was probably only a few minutes, she heard the door squeak open. She had no time to think before he grabbed her and pushed her down hard against the mattress. Instinctively she struggled, kicking and grasping for any part of her attacker. He laughed, low and mean, and pressed his full weight on top of her, his voice menacing in her ear.

It was everything she had fantasized about. Except that life isn't fantasy. It hadn't occurred to them that his first pounce might knock the wind out of her. She tried to keep playing along, but had to call a "time out" after only a minute or so. Struggling had turned out to be more of an aerobic activity than she expected.

He stopped immediately, holding her, stroking her neck and shoulders soothingly as she curled up to catch her breath.

"Are you okay?" he asked, when her breathing sounded normal again.

She nodded, inhaling deeply. "I'm sorry," she whispered.

He shushed her apology with a kiss. "Do you want to stop?" he asked.

"No, no," she assured him. "No, I'm fine. I want to keep going."

"Good," he growled, pulling her against him spoon-fashion and slipping an arm around her to cup her breast. "Because I've been looking forward to this for a long time." He squeezed his hand around her flesh, and she gasped in surprise and pain. And desire.

"You've been teasing me for months, you slut," he whispered. "I've seen you walking around in those tight shorts, wiggling your ass at me."

"No," she moaned, "I don't know what you're talking about. I never...."

"Oh yeah," he continued. "You've been asking for it, and now I'm gonna give it to you."

He pushed her down onto her back, his intimidating figure looming over her. His face was close to hers, his body pinning her to the bed. She could feel his erection, hard and ready against her.

"Please," she begged. "You can't do this. My husband will be home any minute."

The barest hint of a grin penetrated his sinister expression, but only for a moment. "Don't lie to me, bitch," he snarled. "I've been watching this place, and I know your husband is away."

"No," she whispered, impressed with the authentic-sounding desperation in her own voice. "No, please. I swear, he'll be home soon."

"Save your breath," he said. "You're all alone, all mine. And we're going to have a good time together, aren't we?" He stretched a hand down between her legs.

"Bastard!" she hissed, striking out wildly, her fists flying at his smug voice in the semidarkness.

He laughed and caught her wrists in his hands almost effortlessly, then yanked the nightgown up and off, baring her to the waist. Before her shriek of outrage died away, he had hauled her off the bed onto the floor at his feet.

She found herself on her knees on the carpet. Her intruder pressed his knees on either side of her, pinning her arms at her waist and jamming her up against the side of the bed. Her face was level with the bulge in his tight jeans, and even though it was out of character, she couldn't resist rubbing her cheek against the rough fabric. He felt so damned good, all muscle and heat.

A low chuckle came from above her. "See, I knew you were just a little slut. You can't wait to get your mouth on my cock, can you?" he jeered. "I bet those panties of yours are soaked just thinking about what I've got for you."

She wrenched her shoulders trying to get loose, but he just laughed louder and grabbed her by the hair.

"Oh no you don't. You're not going anywhere." His other hand reached for his zipper, and in another moment he was stroking his exposed cock only inches from her face. She tried to pull away, but his hand was still tangled in her hair. The head of his cock came closer until it was rubbing over her lips, and he was muttering, "That's right, you're going to take it all. Open your mouth, little girl."

She whined, "No!" through clenched teeth, and bucked so violently that she nearly got free. He slammed her back against the bed.

"I don't like the word *no,*" he barked. He gripped a nipple, pinching it between his thumb and finger, making her screech. "Are you going to be good?" he asked. To punctuate his question, he pinched again and gave her nipple a cruel twist. She gritted her teeth stubbornly and flattened herself back against the bed.

He changed tactics, and began to stroke her face lightly. He spoke quietly, almost soothingly. "This will be much easier for you if you cooperate. Will you be a good girl?"

She deliberately looked up into his eyes. "No," she said softly.

A stinging pain blossomed on her cheek, and she was stunned to realize that he had slapped her. He knew she had obsessive fantasies about being slapped, but he had never felt comfortable doing it. This stranger in her husband's body both excited her and scared her silly.

"I told you," he growled, "I don't like that word."

She was whimpering now, but he ignored her, pulling her forward and thrusting his cock between her lips. She surrendered to the moment. She had always loved the feel of him growing bigger and harder in her mouth, loved running her tongue over every inch of him, loved teasing him to insanity. But her tormentor had no patience for niceties like that—he shoved himself inside her as far as he could, holding her head, fucking her face roughly the way she had always imagined.

She tried to do what he wanted, but all too soon she had to

pull away, desperate for air. He gave her only a moment before he dragged her back to him, pushing his hips forward to plunge himself even more deeply into her mouth. When he relaxed his grip slightly, she took advantage of the opportunity and jerked her head violently away from him.

"I didn't tell you to stop," he snapped, raising a threatening hand.

She was breathing in big gasps. "Fuck you," she hissed through gritted teeth.

His eyes gleamed. "So that's how it's going to be, is it?"

To her surprise, he did not slap her. He let go of her and zipped his pants up. Before she could take advantage of her freedom, he pulled her up from the floor and onto her back on the bed, his solid body crushing her underneath him.

"You don't want to suck my dick?" he asked, in an ominous tone. She shook her head, trying to stay focused on resisting, but distracted by the pressure of that wonderfully familiar body against her.

Quick as a flash, he produced a piece of rope from his pocket and bound her wrists together. Her head had somehow ended up at the bottom of the bed, which added to her disorientation. He yanked her bound wrists up and tied them swiftly to the bars of the footboard, leaving her body exposed and available to his roaming hands.

"Well, that's fine," he remarked. "There are plenty of other things I like just as much."

He slapped her breast and she yelped. Over and over he smacked her, stopping to pinch and squeeze and twist, alternating with caresses until she thought she would go mad. Being tied made it almost impossible for her to struggle, and she imagined that she could actually feel the adrenaline pouring through her veins.

"Are you going to do what I tell you?" he asked, and she shook her head.

The click of a knife unfolding startled her. Her eyes opened wide as the blade in his hand traced its way up from her belly button, just barely brushing her skin, sending shivers through her.

"Knives are dangerous," he had told her when they had planned the encounter. "If you're fighting, it would be easy for me to slip and accidentally cut you." So she hadn't expected this. But then, she hadn't expected to be bound, either.

Lightly, almost idly, he traced one nipple with the tip of the blade. She couldn't help but moan. She knew that knives aroused him powerfully—almost as powerfully as they aroused her. And when the blade moved up to rest against her soft neck, she found herself looking into a pair of dark, utterly serious eyes. Her breath caught hard.

"What about now?" he asked calmly.

In her mind she was shaking her head, but she couldn't do that, not while there was a sharp edge at her throat. She had to stay absolutely motionless.

"Do you have something to say?" he inquired.

"I...I'm...." She labored to get words out. Her heart was pounding, from the excitement, the heat, the fear.

"Yes?" he demanded, increasing the pressure of the knife slightly, just enough for her to feel the tip dig into her skin.

"I'll do whatever you want," she gasped. "Just don't hurt me." Her cunt contracted as she finally said those fantasy words out loud.

He smiled. "You will do whatever I want," he said. "And maybe I won't hurt you too badly." She felt the knife's pressure release, but before she could react, he warned, "Don't you move one inch." It took a massive effort for her to obey, especially with his fingers trailing down her torso again.

"That's a good girl," he murmured, pinching her inner thighs, then spreading her legs apart and cupping her through her soaked cotton panties.

"Oh god," she whispered. "Please...."

His fingers were agonizingly slow, teasing her, making her wriggle in her bonds. He stroked her pussy lips through the fabric, delicately, lightly, pushing her legs even wider apart when she tried to bring them together. She could barely speak.

"Please don't," she managed to gasp. "Don't touch me, please, not there."

"What?" he asked sharply. "You don't want me to touch you there?"

He flipped the knife out of his pocket again, bunched the fabric of her panties up in his fist, and with two quick slices he cut through the cloth and tossed it away. Without a word he pulled her pussy lips roughly apart, fondling her callously, and smirking when he discovered how wet she really was. She ground herself against his hand, moaning aloud as he pinched her clit and plunged his fingers deep inside her.

"I'll touch you any damned place I want," he informed her. "In fact, you're such a hot little thing that I think I'm going to fuck you."

"No!" she shouted, trying hopelessly to twist away from him. "No! Please! I have money; you can have all of it. Just don't, please don't...."

He smiled to himself. There was probably about ten dollars in her wallet. Not enough to rescue her, even if either one of them wanted her to be rescued.

"I don't want money," he said coolly. "I want *you*."

He had put the knife back in his pocket, so she decided to try one last dramatic gesture.

"Let me GO!" she shouted, kicking out hard on the last word, and connecting with his thigh. His grunt of pain was very satisfying, although she knew she would pay for it. He cursed aloud, temporarily ignoring her as he rubbed his abused leg, while she struggled uselessly to get free.

"You still haven't learned your lesson, have you?" he observed.

He flipped her easily onto her stomach. The ropes were tighter around her wrists that way, and when he rested his weight on her legs, she was completely immobilized. He ran a finger up her bare back, making her shiver, and then locked his hand into her hair. His other hand came crashing down on her upturned bottom, spanking her again and again, making her howl and kick. The blows came fast, without mercy, until she was breathless and sobbing, begging him to stop, promising him anything. His hand thrust unexpectedly between her thighs and came away with incontrovertible evidence of her continued arousal.

Infuriatingly, he chuckled.

Sliding on top of her, he pressed the front of his jeans firmly against her ass, pinning her beneath him, letting her feel his erection through the denim.

"You know what I think you really need?" he hissed into her ear. "I think you need to be fucked in the ass."

She froze, feeling genuine fear for the first time. They had never done that. He couldn't be serious. He was just trying to scare her. Wasn't he?

"Yes, I think that's exactly what a little slut like you needs."

Every muscle in her body was paralyzed. He must know it, must be able to feel how panicked she suddenly was.

"What's the matter? Don't tell me a prick tease like you has never had it up the ass before?" His fingers disappeared back inside her, inflaming her in spite of her fear. Then to her dismay, he pried her cheeks apart and slipped one wet finger easily into her warm back passage. She was shaking her head, her cry anguished, almost shamed. It felt good, very good, and she was so hot, and so scared at the same time; she didn't know if she wanted him to stop or not.

"See what happens to bad girls who don't do as they're told?" he asked, continuing to stroke the soft flesh deep inside her. "Just imagine how it will feel when it's my cock inside that tight little hole."

She was moaning and squirming back against his hand, unable to help herself.

"Please," she whispered almost inaudibly, "please, don't."

"No? So you'd rather I fucked your hot little cunt than your ass?" he asked, abruptly jerking his fingers away and pressing his knee between her legs against her aching pussy. When she didn't answer right away, he pulled her cheeks apart roughly, and she shrieked.

"Yes!" she begged, "Anything but that, anything!"

"Then tell me," he whispered fiercely, sliding on top of her again. "Tell me that you want it."

She could feel his hardness through the layers of his clothing. She groaned and tried to hold out, tried to conceal how badly she wanted him. He thrust hard against her ass. "Tell me," he insisted. "Tell me right now, or you know what will happen."

She surrendered. "Do it, you bastard! Fuck me! I want you to. Please fuck me," she begged.

He had his cock out before she even finished saying it. Unable to wait any longer, he grasped her hips and pulled her up onto her knees, plunging deep inside her warm wetness. Her hands still tied, she bucked back at him, all pretense of resistance abandoned.

He drew her back hard, wrapping his arms around her waist

and driving into her faster, groaning in his pleasure; she was sure that sex had never been this intense before. When he reached around to squeeze her clit, she exploded in blissful starbursts, grinding back against him, her screams mingling with his.

It seemed like a long time before she had the energy to open her eyes, and when she did, she felt him solid and reassuring beside her. His voice was no longer menacing. “Man, this is harder than it looks,” he murmured. “I loved every minute of it, sweetheart, but I’m fucking exhausted.”

“Fucking exhausted is right,” she grinned, curling up in his arms.

They both fell asleep smiling.

THE FIRST STROKE

Erica Dumas

He's been waiting for this moment. He's been begging for it. If it hadn't been for the vagaries of the U.S. Postal Service, he would have had it weeks ago.

The second he sees it, his eyes go wide and his cock starts to stiffen. Then again, maybe it's that I'm not wearing much else—naked except for the harness—or maybe it's the knee-high stiletto boots; those were a specific request, too. Those I bought on Haight Street, for way too much money, I thought at the time. But when I see the way his cock stiffens, his eyes flickering from boots to my cock to my breasts to my face, then back again, several times each second, it seems—well, I know it wasn't too much money at all. I know I would have paid more, because this moment, like the commercial says, is priceless.

I walk slowly over to the edge of the bed, looking him up and down as he looks at me. His cock is fully hard now, which always makes me wet. But there's plenty more to come that'll make me wet, because I'm going to have him in a way he's never been had, in a way I've never had a man.

I don't even have to tell him what to do, but I want to. "Suck my cock," I say, and it's the first time I've ever said it like that. "Suck my dick," sure, it's a common insult, whatever the sex of the speaker. But that word *cock* is so dirty, now, that I just have to use it. "I said suck my fucking cock," I say, and he is on me in an instant, rolled onto his belly so he can lean over the edge of the high bed, placed—as I've discovered numerous times when he was the only one in the bedroom with a cock—right at crotch level.

Of course, the six-inch heels equalize the height difference between us, even if they make me slightly less stable.

His mouth opens wide and he takes in my cock, sucking it. Just a small one—we wanted to start with a reasonable size. But long enough to make him gag a little, as he attempts to deep throat on the first stroke.

"Not much of an experienced cocksucker, are you?" I ask him. Seeing him blush is delicious. His lips come back to the head and he licks it all over, lavishing affection on the realistic silicone appendage. I grab his hair and push him more fully onto my cock. "Real dominants," he'd said, "make me suck it." Not exactly "force me," but "make me," which sends a shiver through his body and makes him suck me with sudden urgency. His lips move up and down on the shaft, covering the ridged cock with glistening saliva. I moan softly. As if it were a real cock, which at the moment it feels like. I could swear I can feel his tongue working on it. Especially when I start to move my hips.

He gags again when the head hits the back of his throat. I thrust deeper. He chokes and pulls back. "Turn over," I tell him. "Spread your legs."

He slides his mouth off my cock and rolls over. I make a "turn-around" gesture with my finger, and he obediently does it, spreading his legs so his knees are bent at the edge of the bed. I reach out and take his cock in my right hand, caressing it at first and then jerking it while I stroke my own cock with my left. Something about the juxtaposition feels good. When I press down just so on the dildo, I can feel the base of it against my clit. I press harder and moan. His cock gives a little pulse. I want him. I want to have him, the way only a woman can have a man.

I reach out to the nightstand for the lube. I drop the bottle onto his belly, and he breathes hard, knowing exactly what's coming. He looks a little scared, his eyes roving over my cock.

"It's not like you didn't ask for it," I say, not sure whether I should have used the flirtatious tone and the little smile or if I should have slapped him across the face and jeered at him. But it doesn't matter, because he's grabbing the lube and drizzling it over the head of my cock. He gets it slick and slippery.

I reach down to grab his legs.

I pull them high up into the air. He is much bigger than me; I couldn't yank him to the edge of the bed if I wanted. But it feels like I pull him, because he slides so easily, pushing himself toward my cock.

When his ass is right at the edge, I dip slightly and guide my cock between his cheeks. I make eye contact with him as I circle the head against his hole, and his look of excitement—seasoned with the slightest hint of fear—makes me hungry.

I move my hips forward and slide into him. He gives a little gasp as the sculpted head goes in. Then he's pushing himself onto me, as I'm meeting his thrust with mine. It goes deep—as deep as it can go—his ass taking me right to the hilt.

I start to fuck him.

My hips move awkwardly at first, acclimating slowly to this new task; usually, of course, it's the other way around. But it's pretty much the same motion, and I thrust into him more swiftly as his ass opens up for me. I reach down and touch his cock, stroking it for a moment, thumbing the head, but I can feel from its hardness and the leaky slickness at the top that if I do much more of that he's going to come. And I want to fuck him for a long, long time.

But I also want to fuck him harder, and when I lean down into him, pressing my body against his, I lose my balance if I take my feet off the floor. So I reach out and grab his wrists before I put my feet back down. I press his hands to my tits, and he fondles them while I fuck him. He pinches the nipples gently and I swear if he just rubbed them a little I could come.

After thirty, forty, maybe fifty thrusts, he's increasingly uncoordinated. I lean back and he lets go, my nipples still tingling from his pinches.

He's groping at the bed, now, not sure what to do with his hands. Finally he slips one finger into his mouth and bites it, in a bizarrely girlish gesture. That makes me fuck him harder. He arches his back on the bed and now both hands are digging into the satin comforter. His head rolls back and his moans grow louder. I fuck him faster.

His cock pulses, its muscles tightening with each thrust I give him. I can't resist any longer. I reach out to grab his cock and stroke it.

His head rolls wildly. He makes eye contact with me and I know it's imminent. I know so well how to jerk him off, except my cock's never before been deep in his ass when I'm doing it. Watching it fascinates me. I love to see his cock pulsating, his come jetting onto his belly as he moans. When he comes, now, he moans louder than ever, and the half-dozen streams coat his belly and chest. I fuck deep into him while he finishes, and he's shivering with pleasure.

I don't slide out of him for a long time, just caress his soft cock and run my fingers through the come all over his belly. When I do slide out, he gives a little gasp. I unbuckle the harness and let it fall around my ankles, my glistening cock projecting obscenely between the pointy patent-leather toes of my stiletto boots. I climb onto the bed and kiss him, feeling the slickness of his cooling come all slippery between us.

His mouth is ravenous, which tells me what he needs. A woman with a cock, of course, is what he asked for. But even without the cock, I'm still in charge, and I want to come. I spread myself on the satin comforter and his mouth is against me, servicing me again—this time my clit, licking me in just the way he knows will make me come. I grip his hair, just enough to encourage him, and it's only a few minutes of his expert tonguing before I come, hungrily, not realizing until I've finished coming that I've done the same thing he did—slipped one finger into my mouth and bitten it, girlishly.

I draw him up onto me, kissing him and tasting my sex. I cup my fingers around his asscheeks, touching his hole, thrilling to the feel of where I've just fucked him.

Which is when I realize that he's hard, again, already. It doesn't take much coaxing to get him inside me, and as he slides in, from the first stroke I have a new appreciation for the experience—having now been on the other side for the very first time.

The first of many such experiences, I'm sure. When he comes, I pull him deep inside me and sigh. His kisses taste like me, and his cock feels better than ever before.

ERIN'S RULES

Erin Sanders

1. When I am in the house, I am naked. I must remove all my clothing when I come home. The only time I'm allowed to put it back on while I'm home is if someone comes to the door who wouldn't understand or doesn't need to understand my status—a delivery person, neighbor, or friend who doesn't know that I am a slave. Then, if it is warm outside, I put on a very tight pair of shorts and a crop top, without bra, panties, or shoes. If it is cold outside, I put on a very tight pair of white sweatpants, a tight white thermal undershirt, and a pair of fur-lined slippers, with no bra or panties. The shirt must be light enough to reveal my nipples and areolae underneath.

2. I shave my pussy each week. Immediately after shaving, I masturbate to orgasm, to remind me that what pleases Master pleases me.

3. I wear only skirts and shorts. I am not allowed to wear slacks or jeans.

4. I do not wear underwear. As my breasts are small, I also do not wear a bra. If my nipples become visible while I am in public, I may not cross my arms to hide them.

5. I will be wet at all times, so that Master may fuck me whenever he wants. If I am not sexually aroused, I will make sure that my pussy stays wet with lubricant.

6. I am not allowed to sit on the furniture at home. I may kneel or sit cross-legged on the floor. If I lie on the floor, I may only lie face down and must keep my legs spread.

7. When I am at home, there will be pornography playing on the television unless guests are over. Master has selected an assortment of DVDs that are acceptable for me to watch. I may not watch anything else without his permission.

8. When Master returns home after being away, I will greet him at the door on my knees and offer him oral gratification. If he chooses, he may use me right there in the hallway, with the door still open if he so wishes.

9. When we are together for the evening or on the weekend, I will ask Master each hour if he would like oral sex. If he says yes, I will give it without hesitation.

10. Before I make Master come with my mouth, I will ask him if he wishes to come in me or on me. If he wishes to come in my mouth, I will swallow. If he wishes to come on my face, I will

not wipe it off until he instructs me to.

11. Before bed each night, I must ask Master's permission to occupy his bed. If he withholds it, I will sleep on the floor next to his bed.

12. When Master has a male houseguest who understands and accepts my status, I must offer him the same obedience that I give Master. On entering the house, he will be greeted by me on my knees and offered oral sex. For each hour that he is in the house, he will be offered oral sex, and if he accepts, I will provide it without hesitation, up to and including his orgasm, and I will then swallow his come.

13. Master may allow any man or woman he wishes to use me in whatever way he deems appropriate.

14. Master may take whatever photographs or videotapes of me he wishes, and may share them in person or electronically with anyone he wants. Master may also instruct me to write erotic letters or emails to anyone he wishes, to whatever specifications or scenarios he assigns, and I will do my best to make them erotic, exciting, and interesting. I will sign my name.

15. When Master is traveling, I will call him at least once per day and offer him phone sex. If he accepts, I will do my best to invent a scenario that excites him.

16. When I am traveling, I will call Master at least three times per day from a private location and ask him if he wishes me to masturbate. If he says yes, I will do so while he listens, and will tell him exactly what I am fantasizing about, in detail.

17. Master may pierce or tattoo any part of my body he wishes, in any manner he chooses.

18. Master may instruct me to write down the rules for my behavior and publish them under my real name or a pseudonym, as he sees fit.

19. I will always love Master no matter what he does.

20. Master may love me as he sees fit.

Idyll

Teresa Lamai

"Fatima, just take it. You don't have to ask."

There was fresh sweet bread on the table and for the first time in months I felt hunger sharply. My new housemate Goran got angry when I asked for some. I was still learning that Goran prides himself on not owning anything, not wanting anything. I didn't notice Amel smirking in the corner until he was suddenly standing next to me. He twisted off one end of the bread and said, "Come see the garden."

Goran and Amel are the only Croatians living in this tiny house by the cemetery in Zagreb. They came to the city for the university, but their families can't afford the new tuition. So instead they load trucks and work in Peace and Anarchy, a youth center built in an abandoned gasworks. The rest of us are from Bosnia. I should say we're refugees from Bosnia, being here in Zagreb in a strictly provisional sense, on our way to Pakistan or Germany or the United States.

As the only girl, I have my own room. Slavica, an older woman my mother had known, was living in the front room with her father and her baby son when I arrived; they've since been relocated to Austria. There will most likely be more refugees to take their place but for now it's just the three of us. Amel and Goran live in the larger upstairs bedroom, and I in the smaller bedroom.

Just seven months ago, it became clear I had to leave Bosnia. My parents were gone soon after the sniping started, and my brothers got German visas for their families. Sarajevo is like a dream now. I can't always separate the reality of what happened from the rumors that consumed us like a collective psychosis.

I may eventually join my brothers in Germany. I may get a visa for the U.S. I may stay forever here with Amel and Goran.

The sun here is stronger, more Mediterranean. Even in the early morning it's like an ancient power in a limpid, fragrant sky. The first mass is ending at the cathedral across the street and the shaded cemetery is already flickering with plastic memorial candles. The courtyards of the blue-painted Romani tenements next door are filling with children. I'm washing the sheets in our yard. The garden is a late-summer mess of palm trees, kiwi vines, and wild roses. There's no sense in grooming anything, since no one stays here long.

Goran comes out, a fat pastry in one hand, a guitar in the other. His long curls are wet, snaking down his bare back. He puts the guitar on the ground and sits next to me to help. Amel has been out here all morning, simply because, like a sly shadow, he is never far from me. Goran laughs at himself as he wrings one corner of a sheet. His fuzzy thigh presses into my skirt. Warmth on my shoulders and soft pulls at my skull tell me Amel is behind me now. He's braiding grass into my hair, as he likes to do when we're outside.

We sit quietly for a long, long time. Every time the breeze stops, I can almost hear our hearts beating.

I'm in love with Goran because of his generosity and sweetness without limits. He carries his large, masculine frame with a sense of wonder and discomfort, as if he had just grown into it. His wide shoulders make the house seem small. He towers over me. I think he is intent on keeping his round blue eyes clear of unkind thoughts, as if he believes innocence will protect him like enchanted armor. He fed me constantly when I first arrived here, cutting me slices of bread and cheese and asking whether I preferred coffee or chocolate milk or maybe green tea until I burst into exasperated laughter and started smacking him. Our first kiss was a week later, when he came home with a bag of birdseed for me to feed the sparrows outside my bedroom window. As if he expected me to be here forever; I couldn't stand it. I grasped his round cheeks between my palms, drinking in his unsettled gaze for a few moments before touching my lips to his. His startled moans made me wet.

His innocence feels less contrived when I'm pressing into him. I'm teaching him that love is selfish. I grab his ass strongly enough to hurt, digging crescents into the flesh, sometimes leaving tiny scabs. I have never told him I love him but he knows from the way I kiss him, the way I run my tongue over his neck and the warm sweet mounds of his chest. The first time I gripped the base of his hardening cock and nipped at his scrotum, he gasped, "That's good, that's so good," with genuine surprise in his voice. I know it's unbearable for him to lie still when I'm teasing the silky head of his cock from its foreskin, using just my tongue. I tell him to lie still anyway because I want us both to be free from what he thinks he should do. I just want to torture him until he's angry enough to fuck me without thinking, his hands tight on my pelvis, cock scorching through my cunt, both of us transported and beyond hurting.

I love Amel for his black silent eyes that seem to absorb everything he looks at. He is slight and dark, speaking rarely, disappearing into the night when it falls. Goran says Amel seems to always be ashamed. Amel follows me stealthily like a cat as I move through the house, settling in the kitchen when I cook or unexpectedly lying on the carpet beside me when I read. We're not sure where he goes in the evenings.

Nearly every night, I wake up after midnight. The moon has shifted. The air is still. I never hear Amel come home, or open my door, or undress, or pull the covers off the bed. I've never seen him naked in the daylight. His voice is what wakes me first, followed by the smooth glide of his belly on mine. The smoky, sweet smell of his hair as it falls on my forehead. His hands are so painfully delicate on the back of my neck that I forget not to moan.

His skin starts to gleam, slippery with our sweat. He moves slowly as if he were underwater, and the breath is sucked out of me as he writhes, his full weight on mine. I'm fascinated by the slick heat of his body; I press one damp breast into him, then the other, stretching my back to let the arcs of our stomachs kiss. He keeps his hips away from me until this moment. He knows I'll be wet when he lowers his cock to slide against my aching lips, just splitting them to let the scent fill the room. This is when he finally kisses me. He lets me try to devour him with my mouth and my pussy, and he knows that he can do whatever he wants with me.

I move to lock my ankles behind him but he pulls me to the edge of the bed. Kneeling on the floor, he leans into my shaking thighs and laps with astonishing patience, from time to time sucking on the inner and outer labia until they burn under his breath. The heat is in my chest, suffocating me. When he starts to massage my clit with two fingers, I buck and he stops suddenly, moving up my body to kiss me with swollen lips that taste like seaweed and old red wine.

Amel plays this game over and over until just before dawn. When the first birds start singing, he slides himself into me slowly, as if he's afraid he'll be burnt. I'm not sure if I can take it when I first start to come, impaling myself desperately. I don't care anymore about the obscene sounds I'm making; I feel this racing sweetness will kill me if I don't let it out somehow. My cunt clenches tight, pulling on him until he stops, his spine twisting sideways as the come moves through him. He breaks into the exhausted, final thrusts as the sky becomes light.

I let him sleep. I get up because Goran and I always have our breakfast early in the garden. Goran is usually up already, wearing just his shorts, slouching on the moss-covered bench. He puts aside the guitar and holds out his arms to me. His chest is sun-warmed.

Lately there has been no work for them, so they stay home with me all day. We read in the morning, sometimes go to the market to buy flowers or vegetables, and lie in the shady grass all afternoon. The lemon tree is starting to bear fruit. We are not sure how much longer we can go without paying rent.

The third notice came for me today. If I fail once again to report in a timely manner, I'm told, the offer of a U.S. visa will be retracted. I can't finish reading this right now; it's time to make lunch. I drop the letter behind my bed and walk out to the patio.

ABOUT THE AUTHORS

MIRANDA AUSTIN is the author of *Phone Sex: Aural Thrills and Oral Skills* and a coauthor, with Sam Atwood, of *The Toybag Guide to Erotic Knifeplay*. She is a former phone sex worker, graphic designer, BDSM enthusiast, and professional arts advocate. She has a couple of academic degrees, spends too much time at her computer, and lives with her primary partner and a pair of extremely dominant cats. Her website is www.mirandaaustin.com.

ZOE BISHOP is a San Francisco Web designer who has had her erotica published online, though this is her first analog erotica appearance. She doesn't have a website or blog because it's all just too much darn work.

ALYSSA BROOKS is a multipublished author of erotica and erotic romances. To find out more about her books, visit www.alyssabrooks.com; readers can view free short stories there and get more info on joining her e-zine, *Wicked Escapes*, "a monthly treat in your inbox, featuring an escape from a featured erotic author, excerpts, and many extras."

CHRIS COSTELLO lives in Arizona and has written for such small press zines as *Lunatic, Prestidigitation,* and *Smut Parade.*

ERICA DUMAS has written for *Good Vibes Magazine,* the *Sweet Life* series, and numerous books in the *Naughty Stories from A to Z* series, including, most recently, *Naughty Detective Stories from A to Z.*

A. D. R. FORTE's erotic short fiction has appeared in the anthology *Awakening the Virgin 2* and in *Scared Naked* magazine. She lives in Texas and tries to avoid daylight hours as much as possible.

BJ FRANKLIN has been writing erotica for only a year, so was thrilled to have her story "The Wheels on the Bus" published in March in *Good Vibes Magazine*. She is a member of the Erotica Readers and Writers Association. Her story "The Lady-Killer" appeared on the ERWA website and has been accepted by Sage Vivant and M. Christian for publication in spring 2006 in their *Amazons* anthology. The author enjoys swimming, loves *Star Trek Voyager,* and in her spare time studies medicine at a university.

DEBRA HYDE's inner introvert struggles against what she's come to call her own accidental exhibitionism, but it has no problem when it chooses to express that exhibitionism through the written word. You can find her most recent erotica in *Best*

Lesbian Erotica 2006; *The Good Parts: Pure Lesbian Erotica*; *Stirring Up a Storm: Tales of the Sensual, the Sexual, and the Erotic*; *Best Bondage Erotica 2*; and both volumes of *Naughty Spanking Stories from A to Z*. When she isn't dreaming about (or engaging in) sex, she's writing about it at her long-running blog, Pursed Lips, at www.pursedlips.com.

KAY JAYBEE is a thirty-something medievalist living in the Grampians of Scotland. She juggles two jobs, two daughters, and as much writing as ahe can squeeze into an average day—providing that black coffee and cakes are at hand. She has recently had her erotica featured on several websites, and she's looking forward to the future publication of a poem (nonerotic) in a book called *Mixed Emotions*.

CAROLINA JOHN is married, with an assortment of pets. She lives in Stourbridge, England, and her illustrated anthology of poetry has just been published by Kates Hill Press.

KC is the pseudonym of a San Francisco Bay Area erotic writer who believes that some things are too naughty even to use the regular pseudonym.

TERESA LAMAI lives in the Pacific Northwest. She started writing in 2003. Her stories appear in *Best of Best Lesbian Erotica 2*, *Best Women's Erotica 2006*, *The Mammoth Book of Best New Erotica*, and *Dying for It: Tales of Sex and Death*. A former dancer, she's recently completed a collection of dance-inspired erotica, entitled *Swayed to Music*. She's working on her first novel.

TSAURAH LITZKY loves to write sexy stories. Her erotica has appeared in more than sixty publications, including *Best American Erotica* six times. In 2004, her erotic novella, *The Motion of the Ocean,* was published by Simon & Schuster as part of *Three the Hard Way,* a series of erotic novellas edited by Susie Bright. Litzky teaches erotic writing at the New School in Manhattan. To find out more about her, check her website at www.tsaurahlitzky.com.

DARA PRISAMT MURRAY's poetry and prose appear in *Intimate Kisses, Velvet Heat,* and *The Mammoth Book of Women's Fantasies* as well as on CleanSheets.com. Her favorite activities, all beginning with the letter *S,* include, first, the obvious, followed by singing, swimming, and shopping. She won't divulge her day job for fear of sullying her reputation as a hot New York City cabaret performer and a proud writer of erotica.

HEATHER PELTIER's work has appeared in *Eros Zine, Good Vibes Magazine,* the *Sweet Life* series, and the *Naughty Stories from A to Z* series. She is at work on a book of poetry and several longer works.

JULIA PRICE has written for a wide variety of anthologies, magazines, and websites. She lives in West Hollywood with her lover and too many cats, and is presently at work on a novel.

AYRE RILEY has written for *Down and Dirty, Best Bondage Erotica 2, Naughty Stories from A to Z* volumes 3 and 4, and *Slave* (edited by N. T. Morley). She lives in Hollywood, Florida.

THOMAS S. ROCHE's novel *The Panama Laugh* was a finalist for the Horror Writers' Association's Bram Stoker Award. Roche's other books include the *Noirotica* series of erotic crime anthologies and four collections of fantasy and horror. A prolific blogger, Roche writes regularly for TinyNibbles.com, BoiledHard.com and many other blogs.

ERIN SANDERS is a midwestern submissive who has recently found steady work in comedy writing. She resides with her longtime partner near Saint Louis, Missouri.

J. SINCLAIRE is a Toronto-based writer by profession but erotic by nature. A firm believer that sex and masturbation are both healthy and necessary, she considers it her civic duty to write smut. The rest is up to you.

ABOUT THE EDITOR

VIOLET BLUE (tinynibbles.com, @violetblue) is an award-winning author and editor, CNET reporter, CBSi/ZDNet blogger and columnist, a high-profile tech personality and one of *Wired*'s Faces of Innovation. She is regarded as the foremost expert in the field of sex and technology, a sex-positive mainstream media pundit (*MacLife,* CNN, "The Oprah Winfrey Show") and is interviewed, quoted and featured in outlets ranging from ABC News to the *Wall Street Journal.*

Blue was the notorious sex columnist for the *San Francisco Chronicle.* She has been at the center of many Internet scandals, including Google's "nymwars" and Libya's web domain censorship and seizures—*Forbes* calls her "omnipresent on the web" and named her a *Forbes* Web Celeb. She headlines and keynotes at global technology conferences, including ETech, LeWeb, SXSW: Interactive and two Google Tech Talks at Google, Inc. and received a standing ovation at Seattle's Gnomedex.

The *London Times* named Violet Blue "one of the 40 bloggers who really count."